Helmar Neubacher

ADOLF HITLER »THE EVIL«

– and the Revenge of the Billy Goat of Leonding

Novel

Helmar Neubacher, born on the 6th of April, 1940, in Sakuten, District of Memel, formerly Germany

Director of Studies (retired)

Graduate Engineer for marine engineering – Qualification CI. Deployment on all oceans and from engineer-assistant to chief engineer

University degree: Instructor for trade and industry with the subjects metal- and machine engineering and social sciences with special focus on political science

Subsequently: Technical instructor and coordinator at vocational education institutions as well as head of technical seminars for teachers with practical aspect work

Publications so far:

Adolf Hitler »Das Böse«
– eine Kindersünde mit schwerwiegenden Folgen
ISBN: 978-3-8448-8977-2

CHEOPS-PYRAMIDE
gebaut mit den eigenen BARKEN
Lösung des Jahrtausendrätsels:
MASCHINEN des HERODOT + KRAFT des WASSERS
ISBN-13: 978-3-8370-6236-6

Das RAD des PHARAO
7 Vorbedingungen für den Bau der Cheops-Pyramide
DER BAU BEGINNT
ISBN: 978-3-8370-2310-7

VERMÄCHTNIS des HERODOT
zum Bau der
CHEOPS-PYRAMIDE
Jahrtausende altes Mysterium gelüftet:
100.000 Mann – Hydrostatik – 230 Steinhebemaschinen
ISBN: 978-3-8391-1486-5

PRINZESSIN DER HERZEN
– ein Drama im Spiegel der Galaxien
ISBN: 978-3-8423-5222-3

WIR DAS VOLK – Bruch der Schere zwischen Arm und Reich –
eine Streitschrift
ISBN: 9 783744855631

Helmar Neubacher

ADOLF HITLER »THE EVIL«

– and the Revenge of the
Billy Goat of Leonding

Novel

Cover:
Draft and design: Schaduf Book

Bibliographic Information of the German National Library.

The German National Library lists this publication in the German National Bibliography.

Detailed bibliographic data is accessible on the Internet under http//dnb.d-nb.de

Copyright 2018 Helmar Neubacher

Production and Publishers: BoD- Books on Demand, Norderstedt

ISBN: 978-3-7481-8276-4

The story told in this book has been randomly invented. The plot does, however, follow historical, actual events. The reference to the acting, mostly non-fictional persons is deliberate.

Even Though it is a novel, the plot of the book closely follows events from the time of round about 1918 to 1945, in which Adolf Hitler took power and decided the fate of the German people as from 1933.

To document the nearness of the plot in this book to the historical environment, some quotes are used, even though this is not common practice in a novel.

Resemblance with still living or already deceased persons is merely coincidental.

Exempted from this are the following Persons, all being contemporary witnesses:

Adolf Hitler, Rudolf Heß, Herrmann Göring, Joseph Goebbels, Albert Speer, Wilhelm Keitel, Martin Bormann, Heinrich Himmler, Eva Braun, Frau Winter, Heinrich Hoffmann, Angela Maria »Geli« Raubal, Angela Raubal, Ernst Röm, Gregor Strasser, Otto Strasser.

Eugen Wasner, Bruno Kneisel, Dietrich Güstrow (alias: Dietrich Wilde), General von Hase, Judge General Dr. Rosenkranz, Prof. Dr. Müller-Hess.

August Kubizek, Stefanie Isak, Aneliese Zakreys, Dr. Bloch, Prof. Hermann Toppa, Michael Watschinger, Prof. Leopold Pötsch.

President Mobuto Sese Seko.

Open Letter to the following Embassies

Embassy of the Russian Federation
Unter den Linden 63-65
10117 Berlin
and
Embassy of the State of Israel in Berlin
Auguste-Viktoria-Strasse 74
14193 Berlin

Your Excellencies,

in the book presented some very slanderous terms of the time, in which Adolf Hitler was Chancellor of the German Reich or on his way there, are used.

I, the author, a former vocational instructor of the state of Lower Saxony in Germany, and I clearly dissociate myself from the "extremely evil terms" of those times, which solely are to the purpose of the subject of the content of the book.

Even though I, too, have lost my home in »Memelland«, today Lithuania, by the ill-fated 2. World War, I fully agree to the statement of the former President of the Federal Republic of Germany Richard von Weizäcker, who in a general sense said, that the »Victorious Powers« had liberated the German people from the »Monster Hitler« and his »willing helpers«.

The 8th of May 1945, the day of the end of the war, in a speech to the 40th anniversary of the Federal Republic of Germany was called the »Day of Liberation«, because the German people were freed from the contemptuous system of national-socialist despotism.

Yours faithfully

Helmar Neubacher, Author

Contents

Operation »Flight of the Swallow« (Schwalbenflug) –
The death sentence for »Geli« Raubal

The Murderers are coming ––
The end of Hitler's niece »Geli«

The Escalation of »Evil« –
The highly developed people of the »Toranians« in the
Andromeda galaxy anticipate the danger of a 3rd World
War on the Earth of humans in 1944/45
(Author's first person narrative)

Loss of Homeland –
The scourge of war drives a completely innocent child of 4
years of age from the German Memel Territory in 1944/45

Special remark to the author's

"Author's first person narrative"

It may, in the beginning, irritate the reader that with the help of an artificial character in three chapters of the book, descriptions, analyses and evaluations about the events around the dictator Adolf Hitler are given. With this "operation" the author reserves for himself with a so-called "Author's first person narrative" the sovereignty of interpretation over the events mentioned.

Especially the alarming events around the former "Fuehrer" of the Germans can now be assessed from the point of view of a millions of years old people.

The name of the artificial character is "Immo" – a history student of the Toranian people who live 2.5 million light years distant from us humans on a" Far away Earth" (see also pp.11,13).

Remark: In the opinion of the author, this book is not suitable
            for children.

The »Evil« –
The moulding of Adolf Hitler's character

"Who were you, Adolf Hitler?
What were you?

Were you a human being, were you a monster or just merely a human »monster«?

Why were you, Adolf Hitler, so terribly »evil«, that there could be no enhancement for the word »evil« anymore?"

That is a question which in the past many authors and film makers tried to pursue, without delivering satisfactory answers.

The here present book also makes a topic of the »evil« in the former »Fuehrer« of the Germans, combined with the intention of lifting the »veil of anonymity« just a little bit, of the man who achieved within only twelve years to bring such endless suffering over the peoples of the world.

Army Military Court Berlin 1943 –
The trial of Hitler's schoolfriend Eugen Wasner concerning insult of the »Fuehrer«

"You are a scoundrel, because only a scoundrel can behave as rotten as that!

In the extremely difficult and tense situation in which our homeland in August of 1943 finds itself, you stab our whole people in the back – the German people, to which you, at least to this day, belong! You are not only doing it by so called critical comments, but veritably in a mendacious and sadistic way. You stab the man in the back who, in an actually heroic battle untiringly makes heads against the Bolsheviks from the East and the warmongers from the West.

Precisely in the moment of a phase in which the commander in chief of our armed forces – father of our great Arian people – needs every, and be it ever so little, support from every German subject, in this moment of a heroic battle, you, as a soldier under oath, do not stand behind your commander in chief. You are breaking your oath as a soldier by revoking your obedience and insulting our supreme commander in a most malicious way.

You do not, with all your might, support your Supreme Commander, but you dare to denigrate our beloved »Fuehrer« in a most miserable way − and the despicable part of it is:

You chose a really ghostly,
mendacious story

You, the accused, are a scoundrel! That I have to tell you personally before the beginning of the trial, you, who has sullied our holy military tunic.

You have thereby also insulted your former comrades to the utmost who in self-sacrificing are fighting at all fronts at risk of their lives to achieve the final victory.

Do not hope for sympathy, accused,
may the just wrath of the German people
come upon you!
You insidious, despicable scoundrel!
Long live our »Fuehrer«! Heil Hitler! − The trial is opened!"

…..."I, Immo, a boy living on the planet »Tora«, more than two million light years distant[1] from the earth of the humans, am stunned and put off , because it is indeed really quite something, how the judge general as chairman proceeds against the accused − and that even before the actual trial before the Central Military Court in Berlin has begun.

Hereto I do have to firstly introduce myself to the honoured reader: My name is Imhotep, but am called Immo. I am a boy at the age of 7500 years − measured in human years − who finds himself in a longstanding university course.

For the subject history I have for the beginning chosen the recent past, in which the dictator Adolf Hitler moved the fate of the German people on Earth I (see plan in Illustration 1). It began slowly creeping in 1919 after World War I, proceeded through the 1920s, increased in intensity in the 1930s to come to an abrupt conclusion at its climax in 1945.

---

[1] *One light year corresponds to the distance travelled by a space ship in one year at a speed of about 300,000 km/sec − i.e. about 10 trillion kilometres (10 x 10^{12} kilometres) distance*

Some of my readers may already know me from my novel »Princess of Hearts – a Drama as seen in the View of the Galaxies« (German only).

For those readers who do not yet know me, may the following short explanation be added: We on »Tora« are a very intelligent people with a history of development of many millions of years. We call our home planet Earth IV. Earth IV and Earth III (planet of the »Kerstakians«) are situated within the Andromeda-Galaxy. Earth II, the one of the »Keranians«, and Earth I, that of the Humans, lie outside of our galaxy in their own solar systems and over two million light years distant from us »Toranians« (Illus. 1).

…… one of millions of star formations in the infinite vastness of space……

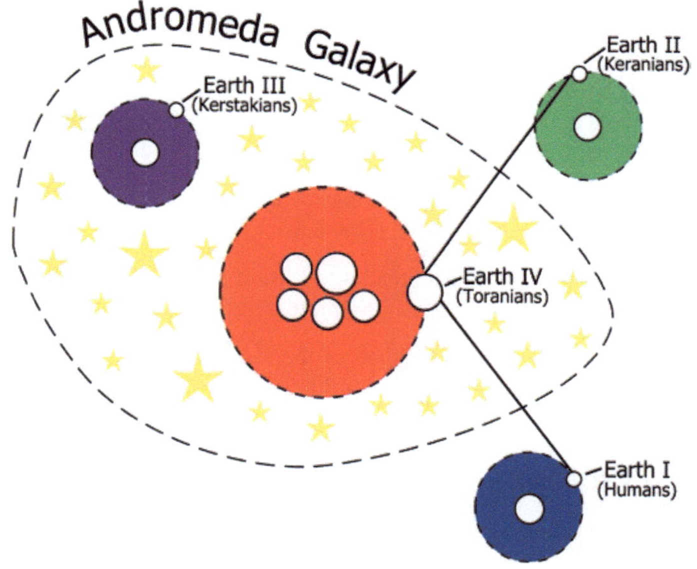

Illus. 1   *Plan – depiction of the Andromeda-Galaxy and the position of four planets, all bearing the name Earth – after a concept of the author.*

The planet »Tora« cannot be recognized from the two far distant Earths with the naked eye. But the huge star cluster – the Andromeda Galaxy – may be seen with the naked eye from Earth I and Earth II, despite the gigantic distances.

We »Toranians« have found out, that only these four planets exist in all of space – four celestial bodies, orbiting one or more suns, with comparable external conditions.

It is really astounding, that we have found no further earth-like structures. After all, there is, all in all, an infinite number of celestial bodies in space.

On the Earth of the Humans a wise man once said that one could estimate the approximate number, if one would count all the grains of sand that there are in the deserts, on the beaches, and on the sea beds and on the land masses – then you would have the approximate number. We »Toranians« have to praise that man with his audacious ideas, because with his comparison to grains of sand he comes very close to the actual number of all stars, planets, satellites and the rest of the celestial bodies.

The four planets shown in Illustration 1, distinguish themselves thereby that on their surfaces similar conditions prevail concerning atmosphere, oxygen, water, gravity, climate etc., thus ensuring that, in the furthest sense, there can exist »anthropoid beings«, animals and plants, too.

I will come back to the point later why Humans are in such a special way interesting to us »Toranians«.

So that you have, honoured reader, a certain picture of our looks, I will add two small sketches of my mother and myself (Illus. 2).

You will probably be astonished of the fact, that we »Toranians« are much prettier than you might expect from the many imaginative drawings and films about aliens. In the imagination of Humans there prevails the presumption that we resemble monsters, just like Humans describe the inhabitants of Mars.

We are certainly an infinite distant species, but insect antlers, predator-like jaws and parts of body that remind you of complicated screw connections, you will not find on us.

Admittedly, we are a bit small, compared to the body size of humans and of the »Keranians«, too. But when you, honoured reader, realize that here every normal child can run the »100 metres« in 3.9 seconds, then we »little ones« are once again very »big«!

I am sitting here in front of my huge plasma TV-screen and am receiving in a matter of seconds pin-sharp pictures of the Earth of

Illus. 2   *Immo, a boy from the planet »Tora« (left) and his mother (right)*
– after a concept of the author.

– the height of body of the grown-ups is about 95cm.

the humans, multi-dimensional before my eye and thus perceived perfectly three-dimensional.

In this case it is about an important historical document of a court trial from days already gone by, that has been recalled into the present especially for me. I will now follow the progress of the trial most exactly, and then draw the necessary conclusions for my studies of history.".....

Before the Central Military Court in Berlin, the Lance Corporal Eugen Wasner, once a school friend of Adolf Hitler's, has to face responsibility in autumn of 1943 – under the threat of being sentenced to death.

And that the accused has nothing good to expect, is again clear at the beginning of the trial in the expression and gesture of those present: Frosty, rejecting and really punishing stares, marked by arrogance and superiority literally go right through him. One can feel the lethal threat coming forth from the side of the command of the court.

"Has the verdict already been passed even before the beginning of the trial?", this question is forced upon the observer.

Meanwhile the accused is sitting slumped in a heap on a bench. He makes a miserable figure, compared with the people on the raised judges' rostrum all actually bristling with brass. On a second, small bench there sits his counsel for the defence in a black robe – flipping through the pages of a thick folder which is in front of him on a tiny table.

The two arms-bristling petty officers are standing immediately behind the accused and his counsel. The machine pistols before their chests, the smart uniforms and their void, absolutely expressionless faces have something threatening coming forth from them. The guards are decorated with the Iron Cross First Class which they are wearing quite conspicuously. One gets the impression that they are not only keeping the accused under surveillance, but his lawyer as well.

"Is the counsel of the defence even at the beginning of the trial to be put under pressure?"

The two arms bristling petty officers are possibly being singled out from the mass of their colleagues. It would certainly be some kind of a military honour to be taking part in this trial.

The accused is of small stature – slender. His uniform has been taken from him and he was stuck into a much too large pair of dungarees. The jacket, too, is much oversize, but allows the view on a light-green jail shirt closed at the neck, which really doesn't seem to fit to the dirty grey, lightly striped flapping dress.

The accused appears totally intimidated. Three months of solitary confinement in the military remand prison in Berlin-Spandau, completely isolated from the world around him, have left their marks. The just on fifty-year-old has deeply engraved wrinkles which enhance his worried expression. Large black rims under the eyes give witness that this man hasn't slept properly for nearly one hundred days and probably hadn't been supplied with all too ample food either. Oversized bald spots of hair receding at the temples amplify the picture of someone mentally worn down.

Detention full of privation is already showing its immense results. The emaciated face and the hanging shoulders and bent back clearly signal:

"I am afraid and I am so terribly alone and altogether helpless against the power of the judges!"

And as if wishing to hope for just a tiny bit of understanding as to the situation of his person, the accused dares a timid gaze around. There are also sitting two writers who are taking everything down for the record, and a third soldier operating a tape-recorder.

In the centre of the event, however, there stand the absolutely grimly looking Judge General as chairman, two army judges as assessors and the court martial senior civil servant as counsel for the prosecution.

Strangely enough, at this moment the accused is not looking in the direction of these four men, but like dumbfounded on a point to their right.

He now begins to shiver, even though it is comfortably warm in the court room. Does the accused actually recognize the danger as not coming from the front but from further to the right?

Exactly; here he sees two men who are not real – who are not sitting there – but still these two people are gaining more and more clearness and distinctness to the accused, weakened and shaken with cold shivers.

"It is from there that the actual attack on me, an unimportant petty lance corporal, comes from. Those two are the dangerous opponents, not the chairman and his three »colleagues of the court«!" he makes his own situation clear to himself.

Eugen Wasner keeps his eyes fixed on that ominous spot with the imaginary men to the right of the people leading the court proceedings.

Now he sees them quite clearly and he recognizes them, too:
The personal aide-de-camp of Field Marshal Keitel and his orderly.

Both are looking gravely and nearly sadly towards the accused – if only their look wasn't so piercing. Their officers' uniforms hung with insignias of rank and medals make them appear huge and overpowering, as in contrast to the inconspicuous accused in his minuteness.

Here the comparison is forced upon you of a huge tiger who has planted himself in front of a tiny little fawn which is shaking with fear and whose weak, spindly legs are just about to cave in.

This comparison with the overpowering tiger, bursting with strength, may well be fitting, because a heavy chain of steel which ties the feet makes a out of the accused a being comparable to the totally intimidated fawn.

On the one side, the bloodthirsty, superior tiger – on the other side the tiny fawn which seems to consist of nothing but oversized, fearful brown eyes – a last call for its mother!

The accused flinches, actually starts: The aide-de-camp of Field Marshal Keitel has suddenly disappeared and so has his orderly!

Eugen Wasner rubs his eyes – unbelievable, he can see neither of them any more.

"I am dreaming or already hallucinating – a mirage in the court room?", Wasner murmurs hardly audible.

"Look this way, accused, and stop that talking! Here is where it's at! Or aren't you even interested in what is happening in court? After all, we are all here only because of you! I am herewith calling you to order!", the voice of the chairman is heard.

The court experienced soldier-jurist has not missed the mental drifting away of the accused. He can't sort it out completely, but he has often experienced the dreaming of the accused, especially in a case about life and death.

"Frequently theses criminals aren't here anymore, but withdraw from reality and are already in the dream-world of their future", the Judge General thinks to himself, while nodding his head as if to agree to himself.

"I am hallucinating", Wasner repeats to himself, but now without moving his lips. No wonder with all that nervous tension and the poor state he is in.

Only yesterday the lawyer had told his client the incredible:

"Field Marshal Keitel has intervened into the pending trial!"

The to lawyer Güstrow well known Judge General Rosencrantz, who is Supreme Judge of the Military Court at the headquarters of the city commander in Berlin, General von Hase, had confided this to Mr. Güstrow. Because of his absolutely outstanding position, Rosencrantz was informed about these, nevertheless top secret, internal matters.

"An extremely threatening Situation!", Eugen Wasner realizes his personal situation, in which even his last hopes begin to dwindle.

16

Just like the tiny fawn he wishes to call for his mother – but where is the mother of the accused? She would of course be consoling support even by her mere presence.

The Mother, Mrs. Wasner, was certainly not permitted to attend. The public is, as common in such cases, excluded – Reason: Jeopardizing of national security!

"Just as well that the Judge General Rosencrantz gave the information to my lawyer on condition of absolute secrecy – good to know where the actual danger for me arises from – but so terribly alarming, too, in its irrefutable consequence:

My school friend Adolf Hitler wants my head!"

"There – there they are again, Field Marshal Keitel's the two »observers to the trial«, the accused murmurs and is no longer surprised by their repeated appearance before his mind's eye, and not as alarmed as before either.

Eugen Wasner can see the two persons quite clearly once again, because he is staring, as he did before, on the hallucination to the right of the presiding judge.

And the two »observers to the trial« assume, of course, a really murderous predominance. They are the recipients of orders of the Field Marshal, who at this time resides in the Headquarters of the Armed Forces, at present in Rastenburg/Eastern Prussia.

In the immediate vicinity of the headquarters, too, is Adolf Hitler.

To there, to the infamous »Wolf's Lair«, Keitel has to report, and from there the known to be weak-willed General gets his orders, because, in the meantime, Hitler has advanced to be Supreme Commander of the Armed Forces.

So it wasn't really surprising, that Keitel – by order of Hitler – had already before the beginning of the trial, given the explicit order to the Central Military Court, to demand the sentence of death for Eugen Wasner. Moreover he pressed to expedite the course of the trial, because a fast end of the trial was demanded by the »highest of places«.

Keitel expressed himself absolutely annoyed about the fact that the counsel for the prosecution had found it necessary, to ask for a medical certificate about the mental state of the accused, which had then been drawn up after urgent reasoning for the petition by Lawyer Güstrow.

…..”I, Immo, am speechless – and my father can't find any words either! He has already been standing behind me for some time, his eyes riveted to the screen of the huge plasma TV – far away from the events happening on the earth of the humans and for both of us, via the TV screen, so very close – just as if my father and I, his son, were sitting in the court room in Berlin-Spandau.

Especially for him it is totally incomprehensible what is happening there in that lawsuit in 1943. For my father on »Tora« the events on that earth are, however, of immense interest.

›You see, my son, from the point of view of a soldier – and I, too, am a four-star-general – an intervention of that kind by the »Fuehrer« Adolf Hitler and his Field Marshal Keitel should be absolutely impossible to occur – in a pending trial.

You'll see, my son, that Hitler is going to kill poor Wasner with his »long arm« via the court. He is murdering his school friend with whom he grew up and spent his childhood in the same place.

Soon you'll get, my son, the surely still missing information as the trial is continued.

»Bloodthirsty Tiger and tiny, helpless fawn« – a really fitting comparison! Eugen Wasner is already lost!‹, my father, as an expert observer, makes his prediction”…..

The court room has whitewashed walls and is sparsely furnished with seats and has just a few tables. The only decoration is a black-and-white Photo of Adolf Hitler on the wall above the chairman – to the left, the swastika flag of the German Reich and to the right an epigram in black print:

WHAT IS JUST MUST STAY JUST!

The public is not permitted, as already mentioned.

<u>Chairman:</u>
"Accused, make your statement as to your person, stand up!"

And the accused explains in a soft voice, that his name is Eugen Wasner, was born in Leonding, formerly Austria, more than 50 years ago, and that he grew up with his now »Fuehrer« Adolf Hitler, had learnt the trade of an accountant and was drawn to the armed forces (the »Wehrmacht«) in 1940.

He had last served in a company of the infantry on the Eastern Front – and that moreover he regrets having told his comrades the

»billy goat story«. It would never have come to his mind to insult or injure his former school friend and now »Fuehrer« and Chancellor of the German Reich. If this impression would have been got, he would like to apologize and ask forgiveness of the »Fuehrer«.

During his short statement, in which his voice comes to falter several times, the accused stands like a scarecrow, with bent back and on sandals that look like weird wooden slippers. Constantly he tries to pull up his much too big trousers, because they hadn't left him with belt and braces. He absolutely makes a pitiful picture, contrasting the other persons in their smart, immaculate uniforms.

<u>Chairman:</u>
"The prosecutor of the »Wehrmacht« has the word, Court Martial Counselor Fersenstein."

"Judge General, gentlemen assessor judges, lawyer. Before us there stands the accused Eugen Wasner. I have now already been counsel for the prosecution for five years, but as clearly as in this case, I have never experienced judicial circumstances.

Several times the accused has already behaved conspicuously, by openly contesting in front of his fighting comrades, the Final Victory.

Stirring war hatred it is called, when someone tries to destroy the courage of his soldier comrades in their battle against the »Russian Subhumans«. The superiors of the accused acted completely correctly and farsightedly to convey these facts to the next disciplinary military level. We owe special thanks to Reserve Lieutenant Meier for revealing this criminal offence.

Already being **high treason** in this case – to be punished with the death sentence – one can simply find no words for the »billy goat story« into which our beloved »Fuehrer« was drawn as a child of only nine years – absolutely absurd!

Were it, in normal times, that one could brush aside this story as having sprung from the »mind of an imbecile«, it is simply not possible in this phase of the war. Moreover, the medical testimonial of the senior surgeon of the Psychiatric Department at the University of Berlin, headed by Prof. Dr. Müller-Hess, proves that the accused is not insane and thus fully criminally liable!

Each and everyone present here has knowledge of this terribly defamatory story, which later I will read out again in full, without going into detail as of now. As the accused has already confessed on several occasions that he has to the deepest insulted and slandered our »Fuehrer«, the admission of guilt lies already before us − and the mentioned crimes call for the **death penalty**!

.....”I, Immo, am sitting on »Tora«, 2,000,000 light years away, but I am petrified with fright − just like the accused who is looking at his lawyer, seeking help. Expectant I am watching the continuing court trial.”.....

<u>Chairman:</u>
“Lawyer Güstrow, you have the word. Refer, however, only to the essential and spare us from insignificant deviations.”

“Judge General, gentlemen assessors, Court Martial Counselor, unfortunately the accused has not to this date retracted this absurd story, but when he is given his say, he will surely tell the high court, that the story is not true, but has sprung entirely from his imagination, connected with the intention, to show off in front of his comrades in battle. In this case, the offence of **undermining the military strength** would no longer apply, because the accused had never intended to slander our »Fuehrer«.

I repeat: It is nothing but the pomposity of a subordinate soldier who had the privilege to have known our »Fuehrer« as a child!

Moreover, the defence asserts mitigating circumstances, because the accused had never intended to insult the »Fuehrer« and Chancellor of the Reich.

The accused deeply regrets the story told to his comrades and again apologizes to his supreme commander Adolf Hitler.”

<u>Chairman:</u>
“Accused, speak now on your own behalf! − But don’t bore us with stories that we have already gone over again and again! To make the whole affair easier for you and for us, too, we will now read out to you what you have already stated for the record several times and have once again signed in the presence of three witnesses two days ago. It is therefore merely necessary to once again confirm the aforementioned text for the record here before the court − it is thus only about the story that you had told your comrades at the Eastern Front three months ago.

Court Martial Counselor, please read out the text of the record, for order’s sake, once again!”

And the counselor for the prosecution immediately begins, his voice not even sounding unfriendly, because the only thing missing is the renewed »Yes« of the accused – the final admission of guilt before the court:

"I had judged the present situation of the war for us all very critically. Especially our own situation I found to be extremely worrying, because we were, in the central part of the Eastern Front, repeatedly engaged with the Russians in rear guard actions resulting in heavy losses.

Our situation was just on hopeless:

- no heavy weaponry, little ammunition
- no relief attacks of neighbouring units
- little food, bad water, no accommodation and no supplies.

The situation was simply disastrous just as was our mood in the unit! To make things worse, winter was once again just ahead, and like a sword of Damocles the defeat of the 6th Army in Stalingrad in January of this year, hung over our heads. Terrified we were thinking of the last 91,000 men of a once so proud army of 300,000 who beaten, louse-ridden, sick, broken, hungry and without warm clothing went into Russian captivity as prisoners of war – simply hopeless, if one considered the defeat of Stalingrad to be already decisive for the outcome of the war.

When I thus stated my concern as a fighting soldier – feeling more like a little warlord who just wanted to contribute something to the entertainment of our little group, one of my comrades requested with the following words to act myself and not just to talk – because they all knew, that I was a school friend from childhood days of our beloved »Fuehrer«.

›Do write to your former school mate. And tell him without much ado what is really happening out here. Your former school friend, our present supreme commander and general, will surely be astonished to hear what it really looks like with his soldiers on the Eastern Front – he, while just studying his maps, certainly doesn't seem to know!‹

I answered him:

»Oh well, our Adolf! He has always been a bit daft from when he was little, knowing that a billy goat had bitten off half of his zippedeus!«[2] [3]

And my soldier comrades were speechless and surprised at this story. I was really incited by the immense interest shown by my comrades – stood in the absolute focus – so that I continued:

*»Yes sir, I was there myself when it happened. It was a bet he made, our Adi, that he would piddle a billy goat into its mouth. When we laughed at him, he said: ›**Come along all of you, we're going to the meadow, there's a billy goat there.**‹*

On the meadow I held the billy goat firmly between my legs, and another friend held the billy goat's mouth open with a stick, and Adolf piddled the goat into its mouth. Just as he was doing that, the friend pulled away the stick, the goat snapped its mouth shut and bit Adolf into his zippedeus. Did our Adi yell terribly and run away howling!«[4]*"*

<u>The Chairman in friendly tone:</u>
"Accused, did you put the just heard text word for word to the record?"

*»*Yes sir, that I had told as a humorous episode from the Fuehrer's youth.*«*[5]

Again the Chairman starts anew, and his voice sounds nearly paternally friendly, but nevertheless with a dangerously lurking undertone. All participants of the trial really sense the treachery and dishonesty of the following question – everyone except the accused! …will he walk into the trap, big as a barn door before him?

<u>Chairman:</u>
"Accused, have you perhaps only invented the story and only told to your friends as a silly joke?"

---

[2] *anglicized version of the Austrian term »Zippedäus«, inconspicuous word for »penis«*

[3] *Dietrich Güstrow, Tödlicher Alltag. Strafverteidiger im Dritten Reich, publishing house Severin und Siedler [1981], p. 134*

[4] *ibidem, p. 134-135*

[5] *ibidem, p. 135*

From the bench of the lawyer only a whistling sound of tension laden air can be heard:

"Everything lost!" is what the whistling sound says.

And the accused answers in a firm voice, his weak, lean body straightens up bolt upright:

»No, I have not just made it up. What is true has to stay true. «[6]

All the participants in the proceedings of the trial look at each other satisfied and smiling, only the accused and his lawyer are not smiling.

They look each other in the eyes – but the four eyes do not understand one another – two pairs of eyes »are speaking« two different languages.

In the courtroom, for on half a minute, you could have heard a pin drop; nothing is heard but the scratching sound of pens of the keepers of the minutes.

<u>Then the voice of the Chairman is heard, saying with a very satisfied undertone:</u>
"I suspend the trial for an hour and a half. Refresh yourselves, gentlemen; we will continue at 2 pm".

….. "My father, the four-star general on the far distant planet »Tora« and I, Immo, his studying son, can well use a break, too.

›Do you see, my son, what a »slimy customer« the chairman is? – He has even built a bridge for poor Wasner, knowing just too well, that the otherwise boastful and opinionated little lance-corporal will not cross over. – He knew right from the start, that Wasner would never admit that he had made up the story and that it was merely a joke!‹

›So the whole thing was only a meaningless phrase, just a load of pretentious waffle – a pun‹, I answer –

›and that Wasner walks straight into the trap!‹" …..

---

[6] *Dietrich Güstrow, Tödlicher Alltag. Strafverteidiger im Dritten Reich, publishing house Severin und Siedler [1981], p. 135*

Two o'clock sharp in the afternoon all participants are back in their seats.

<u>The Chairman opens the second round:</u>
"Court Martial Counselor, please commence with the final summing up for the prosecution."

The prosecutor rises, looking around with an expression of importance on his face, as if more than a hundred listeners were hanging on his every word instead of just the five people present, and he begins:

"Never before has a court trial been this obvious – from the beginning up to here to the very end, I can only repeat myself", and his hereto rather pleasant baritone voice takes a sharp tone, though not getting any louder, but to be compared to the sharpness of a knife. In addition the prosecutor is pointing an outstretched arm and index finger at the accused:

"The accused has confessed his deeds – a crime which in the history of justice is so unique, that we should, after completion of the trial and consequent atonement, forget it as fast as we can. Never before has a supreme commander, neither Frederick the Great nor Napoleon been insulted in such a way, and that by his most inferior subaltern, a lance-corporal.

In the most difficult of defensive battles against Bolshevism a soldier back-stabs his supreme commander! There can be no story more treacherous and slanderous against our »Fuehrer« and Chancellor of the Reich than this. This story is in its repulsiveness at the same time out to shame the whole of the German people – to the shame of the many hundred thousands of combatants on all fronts as well as the home front.

There are thus two crimes inevitably to be punished with the death sentence – namely that of **treachery** and **troop demoralization**.

The accused has therefore made himself guilty of the already 1933 put into force »Special Penal Law« – and in this case »Law of Treachery« and »Special Regulation of Martial Law«. Against such a dangerous individual, as is this here disgraceful lance-corporal, the German people and the »Wehrmacht« have to be protected. Therefore I demand for the accused Eugen Wasner the

Death Penalty!"

Lawyer Güstrow is an experienced specialist for martial law. Already quite often he had, in the last few years in the course of a mounting reign of terror of the national socialist system, been able to bail out the accused – despite danger for his own life.

"But what am I to do in this case?
What can I achieve in the few remaining minutes?

From the very beginning, Eugen Wasner has – before and during the trial – been talking into risking his neck: Like an elephant in a china shop he behaved – now everything is lost – nothing but shattered remains are left!"

<u>Chairman:</u>
"Accused, you have the last word."

Eugen Wasner flinches!

He seems surprised, that he is spoken to once again; he really starts with fright – just as if he had already finished off with everything, and was back to his journey of dreams. But here there is no dream into which one can flee. Eugen Wasner is in the present – and the present is real and hurts – it is lethal!

He is threatened with death – the small accountant brain doesn't can't grasp it any more – death because of a »billy goat story«!

The accused stands up, folds his hands in his lap, positions himself bolt upright – but then the thin, emaciated figure actually crumbles:

sitting slumped in a heap, totally bent on his wooden chair –
nobody comes to his help!

The lawyer can't help either, though sitting at his own table, immediately beside the one of the accused. The defendant is just as pale as his protégé – and he appears even more helpless than he.

"Nothing, absolutely nothing has this thick headed accused contributed to my strategy of defence:

- an invented story
- a youthful escapade that didn't even happen
- a strongly exaggerated story
- to be just once the centre of interest among his soldier comrades
- boast with the fact of having been school friend of the great warlord Adolf Hitler
- to show off with his closeness of juvenile relations
- everything just taken from imagination.

Now: Sincere remorse and huge regret!

Nothing, absolutely nothing has this accused grasped:
He is standing on a cliff, several hundred metres high, – positively aware that the next step will bring him certain death.

But what does this person do?
He doesn't fulfill the saving step backwards.
No, he takes one step forward,
spreads his arms as if he had wings –
smiles and jumps!"

Strange, it seems as if the accused is trying to look at the chairman – or is he actually looking the friend from his youth »Adi« into his so much changed murderous eyes, that are staring at him from the black-and-white photo above the chairman – and the accused states, addressing the picture of the »Fuehrer«:

»For the sake of Jesus and Mary, he did do it, Adi!«[7]

His voice is soft but audible, is getting louder, and the lean Eugen Wasner raises himself up in his miserable slippers and speaks so loudly and clearly that now everyone can hear him:

»But I swear, on my life!«[8]

The chairman is now totally indignant, jumps up, making a cutting short movement of the hand that fits to the absolutely harsh tone of his voice. All that's missing now is the word »scoundrel« as shortly before the beginning of the trial – and he raves:

"That's really enough now! It is absolutely scandalous what this man allows himself to put forth!"

The three military judges stand up and disappear into a conference room.

A mere three and a half minutes pass and the court returns.

Lawyer Dietrich Güstrow knows from experience from many years:

- Time of consulting of the Military Central Court longer than five minutes will result in
  Death passing by!

---

[7] *Dietrich Güstrow, Tödlicher Alltag. Strafverteidiger im Dritten Reich, publishing house Severin und Siedler [1981], p. 139*

[8] *ibidem, p. 139*

- Shorter than five minutes will result in
   **the demand of the penalty stated by the prosecutor to be
   confirmed!**

<u>All participants listen standing up to the verdict of the chairman of
the court:</u>

*» ›In the name of the people‹: The accused Eugen Wasner has
treacherously and in the worst of manners insulted and slandered
Germany's Fuehrer and Chancellor of the Reich. He has hereby
and by other defeatist statements corrupted the military strength of
the German people.*

*He will therefore be punished with the death sentence. [...] The
trial is closed; the accused is to be taken into custody.«*[9]

Awakening and Recognition –
Lance Corporal Wasner sees his schoolfriend
»Adi« demasked as the absolute evil

The accused startles up!

For three days now he has recuperated a little bit, and he is very
calm inside.

For him the episode is closed – the »Story of Eugen Wasner«!

To the accused it has become clear, that the actual topic »Adi and
the Billy Goat« has only contributed a small amount to bringing a
little light into the dubious dark of the person Adolf Hitler – a
darkness which the declared »Fuehrer« of the Germans by no
means wishes to lighten up.

The accused flinches. An unusual noise meets his peace seeking
ear. The door of his cell is ripped open and in comes Lawyer
Güstrow – literally pushed in by two guardsmen.

"Twenty minutes", one of them says curtly. Both turn on their
heels, whip up their right arm and shout as one

"Heil Hitler", and leave.

---

[9] *Dietrich Güstrow, Tödlicher Alltag. Strafverteidiger im Dritten Reich,
publishing house Severin und Siedler [1981], p. 140*

As suddenly as they came, so they have disappeared again. One can only hear the huge key turning in the lock and the lawyer and his protégé are locked up in the extremely small cell.

The lawyer takes a seat on a shaky wooden chair that one of the guards had brought along. Eugen Wasner is, meanwhile, sitting on the edge of his wretched plank bed: only straw and a strongly felted blanket.

Dirty white walls, a hole in the ground where to relieve oneself and a wooden dish that more resembles a pig's trough – filled with brackish water – indicate that a human being lives here.

If one wants to drink, one has to form ones hands to a ladle – a mug or a cup hasn't been granted.

Two metres wide, two meters long and six metres high – that really is a strange measure for a room in which, even if only temporarily, a human being ekes out the last hours of his life. The only »humanely warming« in this cold and inhospitable dwelling is an electric globe which, hanging from a long wire in more than three metres height, throws its sparse light on the rather rough floor covered with cracks and crevices. One gets the impression of the light being thrown to and fro, for bulb and wire are still waving about alarmingly.

A ghostly situation with light and dark constantly following one another, really fitting to the unreality of death row.

The swinging movement of the light were caused by persons entering and leaving, connected with the opening and closing of the cell door – the cell being more like a carpenters' shack made from strong boards and rafters, not screens letting through any air.

They are sitting opposite one another, the experienced counsel of the defence and his client. For one of them it is merely routine, whereas the other one simply can't get used to the new situation in his life.

"Completely helpless in a murderous machine of destruction, from which there isn't even the slightest chance of escape. You're stuck in it as if bound at your hands, feet and neck with chains that are marked by supersized links and additionally firmly fixed to the floor. So the African slaves from over a hundred years ago must have felt, as they were being deported across the oceans to the »New World«", thus, full of bitterness, Eugen Wasner clears his situation to himself in his own mind.

They are sitting closely opposite to one another, the lawyer and his protégé. Even though both of them were pursuing a line of thought for only a few seconds, the time gone by seemed like an eternity.

The lawyer tries a smile which seems strangely tortured, because it's just put on. The convicted prisoner on the other hand, seems quite serious, a bit sad, while looking the person opposite in the eyes.

Lawyer Güstrow produces a heap of files from his black leather briefcase. On the top there is a sheet of paper covered only half with writing, which he passes to his client. For him, a short glance is sufficient, and he hands it back immediately.

Strange, but even though the name »Keitel« doesn't even appear black on white, he knows that the field marshal is the initiator.

It then doesn't even play any part, the refusal of Wasner's plea for clemency including the lawyer's statement of objection has been signed by Judge General Dr. Sack from the Supreme Command of the »Wehrmacht«. The supreme head of the »Wehrmacht« is by no means the Judge General who is bound by directives, but Wilhelm Keitel – that Eugen Wasner had learnt from his lawyer.

Now something entirely unexpected to the counsel of the defence happens: While Eugen Wasner hands back the document back unread, a jolt passes through his lean body and he sits up straight on his miserable plank bed, letting one hear the straw rustle.

Eugen Wasner smiles – smiles for the first time and his smile doesn't even seem artificial. No, this smile gives evidence of a sudden inner calm and balance.

The message says:
"I am not afraid after the storm I've gone through – no, an inner satisfaction takes hold of me and a calm expectation of my fate.

Even though I'm aware of the fact that the terror experienced before the court was like a storm, I foresee, that during the walk to the scaffold, the storm will rise to become a hurricane!"

The convicted prisoner begins to talk, softly but clearly, looking his lawyer into the eyes with composed friendliness – entirely familiar and without any shyness.

Astounding! The more than fifty years old man now speaks in excellent High German, just as if he had completely discarded the Austrian dialect of his Leonding home and perhaps had even totally forgotten it.

"Lawyer", he begins, and his friendly expression of the face gives way to one of deep seriousness.

"Lawyer", he begins anew,

"even though I've never told you, and wasn't able to express it properly, you have helped me very much. You have unselfishly and with all your knowledge and great talent spoken up for me. You have tried really everything – tried everything possible in my difficult and totally messed up case.

You, my lawyer, have never given up, even though also for you it was to clutch at straws. You probably did know all the time, that straws cannot supply any hold. The verdict had already long been spoken. You spoke up for me, untiring, despite of the overpowering opponent, against whom one could achieve nothing, absolutely nothing.

It really startled me when I heard that you, my lawyer, even tried to locate the playmate of Adolf Hitler and me, Bruno Kneisel. It was he who had opened the mouth of the billy goat with a stick, and he would have been the only person who could testify to my story. But your search for the witness of the defence was surely not kept secret from the court, and in the end I was really glad, that Bruno Kneisel could not be found. The authorities of Leonding even testified to his death.

A Bruno Kneisel appearing before the court could never have saved me from the guillotine, but he could have become extremely dangerous to you. I really feared for you, Sir, as your courageous search for Bruno Kneisel would not be hidden from knowledge of the henchmen of the SS[10]. My most sincere thanks to you, Lawyer Güstrow, for endangering even your own life for my cause."

And after a short period of breath taking –a kind of involuntary stoppage – the doomed man continues his speech, much to the astonishment of the counsel of the defence, and now comes to the actual topic, lifting his right arm a bit schoolmasterly and with outstretched index finger pointing to the front. To the lawyer it becomes clear, that now something very important is going to follow, something like a last will and testament:

---

[10] *SS – Shield Squadron. From 1925-1945 a special organization of Adolf Hitler and the NSDAP. Originally founded for the personal protection of Adolf Hitler, it was as from 1933 the most prominent organization of the NAZI regime for terror and suppression.*

"The »friend« who in former days misused his power to piddle a helpless goat into its mouth, today has the power to crush whole peoples. What was perverse then, is perverse today, too, when tens of thousands of, in many cases outstanding, soldiers hang from the gallows or end under the guillotine.

Very honourable fellow countrymen have to suffer a dishonourable death, only because they didn't believe in the »Final Victory« or pilfered, driven by hunger, a chicken or a bar of chocolate.

You see, Sir, he who murders the **school friend**, will murder his **sister**, his **sweetheart**, the **child** and his **people**, too!"

Eugen Wasner forms his hands to a ladle, drinks a bit of the brackish water from the tub standing on the ground and which looks like a pigs' trough and continues with his speech:

"Anyone who does that, must have due hatred on himself!

Is it possibly the fault of a simple domesticated animal – a billy goat?

The leader of a proud people like the Germans has, of course, to be without fault. Just like the whole Aryan race whose ancestors once came down from the slopes of the Himalayan Mountains – as Goebbels and Himmler allegedly had found out – so a mutilated Leader of this proud people naturally doesn't fit anywhere into the doctrine of »perfect Aryans«!

The **»perfect Fuehrer«** of a **»perfect people«** with only half of a penis – and the other half in the stomach of a billy goat, detached in the course of a most deeply perverse game!"

And Eugen Wasner again, as before, raises his index finger and goes on perfectly as in the manner of a school master.

"Just like the then abused billy goat took his revenge on the rake Adolf Hitler, so one day the abused German people will take revenge and bite off the other half of Adolf Hitler's »zippedeus« for his perverse deeds – wait and see, Sir, it will happen in your lifetime, it will be only months at length and the »1000-Year Reich« will be no more!"

After a further short break the convicted lance corporal continues, and Lawyer Güstrow is totally surprised at the farsightedness of the what is put forward – yes actually astonished – of which lines of thought the otherwise somewhat longwindedly reasoning common soldier is capable of. He is capable to immediately heading straight for the essential, to exactly arrange his thoughts and without any long-winded lament.

"That Mr. Wasner, unfortunately is the way it is, and to what you say, I cannot really add anything, in everything you stated, you are perfectly right", the lawyer takes the word in a somewhat husky tone of voice, and he appears extremely helpless, because he couldn't have helped, despite all of his skill and shrewdness, and he knows nothing to put against the words of this doomed man.

After a short break again, the former soldier, now condemned to death, continues in a soft voice – now not looking at the lawyer.

He now has his hands on his lap, looking at the grey, hostile floor of concrete he talks murmuring, withdrawn as if to himself, as if in a soliloquy. Even though the lawyer feels, that even in this phase of the conversation he is talked to directly.

Noticeable is, however, that Eugen Wasner has changed his dialect – he doesn't talk High German any more, but suddenly reverts entirely to the home dialect of his father and mother:

"What a stroke of fate, Sir, the billy goat of 1898 on the meadow of Leonding was sent by god. Only the Lord could achieve to choose the right one from all of the millions of »zepedeuses«. He punished the only person in question with horrible results:

- extreme bodily shame
- complex-ridden for life.

As a result the »perfect Aryan« becomes a »perfect cripple«.

The billy goat of Leonding acted wisely:
Already a nine year old was to learn the meaning of providence!

I, Eugen Wasner, a deistic Christian, thank my creator for sending this clever animal! Everything happened as predetermined from the beginning – and it may possibly be read in the writings of the great »prophet« Nostradamus.

As planned in wise foresight, providence came into action as overriding power – and providence chose the only person in question for this bodily mutilation – the person »Hitler« – who had as a child already been evil and who as an adult enhanced the »evil« until it could only be called »diabolical« and after which there was no possibility of further enhancement!"

And the condemned man smiled again, literally beams at his lawyer, just like a little child proud to have learnt another new word.

He lies down on the plank bed, stretches his legs, while the straw rustles anew, doesn't even turn his back on the lawyer, closes his eyes and immediately begins to snore.

The insignificant lance corporal Eugen Wasner is sleeping for the first time in 100 days. It is the sleep of a person who, at the end of his life, is quite satisfied with himself and has straightened things out – deeply, soundly and relaxing! There is even no need of a dream, for the sleep is dreamlessly deep as if the sleeper were relieved from a more than great load and free from all earthly discord!

The restful sleep mirrors in his totally relaxed facial expression:

"The heart of the insignificant soldier from the middle part of the eastern front is free!"

Lawyer Güstrow is speechless! After some moments, however, he too experiences something like peace of mind. The credo of Eugen Wasner in a better future had settled in him, had created a spark.

Lawyer Güstrow looks at the smiling face of the snoring doomed man. He has never experienced anything like this.

"An extremely unusual situation in which I find myself", he thinks – and smiles, too!

The two guards who have just entered look at each other in disbelief, because of the surreal situation in that cell contemptuous to humanity.

Never have they encountered a lawyer leaving his doomed fellow man with a smile. In surprise they simultaneously reach for the machine guns that are hanging before their chests.

"Oh my god, the doomed man is smiling, too, – and snoring so terribly loud – how audacious!"

Both of them are already beginning to shout an order, but they pause, because the lawyer is making an appeasing movement of the hand.

"Do let him sleep!", the hand demands.

"What a man is this, this insignificant lance corporal Eugen Wasner", the experienced counsel of the defence is thinking, continuing to smile satisfied.

"Even though I am the loser, because I wasn't capable of saving my protégé, I do know now, that I have been defending a winner.

This insignificant lance corporal is actually a »really great one«:
- Deistic and uncompromising he wouldn't think of bartering with the terror justice of the 3rd Reich.
- He stuck to the truth of his story and chose death in return – an extraordinarily high price for a small children's story of three nine-year olds!"

The counsel of the defence from a time that is called National Socialism moves and leaves the prison cell. His step is firm and echoes muffled from the inhospitable walls.

The »Why« of Wars –
The viewpoint of the many millions of years old people of the »Toranians« on a far distant »Earth«

..... "I, Immo, the boy on the planet so infinitely far from the event, now have a question directly burning on my fingers:

›Say, father, don't the humans ever learn from their history? Why did Hitler begin that disastrous war in 1939, the one they call the Second World War? Hadn't there been many examples like »Charlemagne«, »Otto the Great«, »Frederic the Great« – all of them bestowed with the honourable title »the Great«, did wage wars without their own people ever getting happier by it.‹

My father, still staring at the huge plasma screen with the pictures from the earth of the humans, has become quite thoughtful at my question, and after short period of reflection answers:

›The question won't be why Hitler didn't learn anything from the wars of the »Great«, but the question is: Will the humans ever learn to better master their future? To date, there is nothing recognizable in that direction.

- The Germans haven't even really begun reappraising the disastrous circumstances of the 2nd World War into which they staggered shouting »Hitler«.
- The book »Mein Kampf« written by Hitler is prohibited.
- At schools, not even everywhere there are curricula telling teachers which contents and topics from the times of 1919 to 1945 are to be conveyed.‹

›Say, father, if I have understood you correctly, the thought of a comparison with a boxer suggests itself. How can a boxer prevail over his opponent, if he hasn't got the chance to study the combat techniques and fights of his opponent before the first meeting?‹

›Exactly, my son, you can only protect yourself from against future antagonists, demagogues and »Hitlers« if the past is taken up without any taboos, illuminated by analysis and the correct conclusions are drawn.

Everything, absolutely everything has to be put to the test, and to be discussed until it is watertight. It is the only way to reveal future »seducers« like Adolf Hitler, yet before they become great and powerful.

Only who knows his past and interprets it correctly, is then able to learn to form his future!

Summarized in short this, my son, may be a little bit of help for you:

- Go back into the past and look for reasons and causes for everything that happened then.

  Only if you know the causes, you will with the help of this knowledge, be able to reach further insight.

Because: New insights lead to necessary new capability of understanding and convictions.

With that you are set in a position to brave any dangers. You can now protect your life and the lives of others, because you no longer belong to the stupid and ignorant ones!

Well, my son, simplified one could say:
Fear not the »yesterday« – not to repeat the mistakes from former days after having drawn the right conclusions – will make the »future« work. One has grown more knowledgeable and creates a »bulwark against the evil«!‹.....

The Guillotine and the Angel of Death are already waiting –
Lance corporal Wasner sees the grotesque face of Hitler between dream and reality

»Tsss…plop…« a strange double sound – not eve loud, more like a short hissing and scratching with the final dull »plop«!

The blade of the guillotine whizzes down – hits the neck of Eugen Wasner! The severed head falls with a »plop« into the about one metre tall wooden barrel which resembles a sawn off wine barrel.

The whore contraption of the killing machine still trembles a bit, for the heavy, shiny, razor-sharp guillotine blade doesn't really fit to the instable appearing wooden construction. The blade is curved at the cutting edge like an Arabian scimitar – and it gleams in the pale light of the sparsely lit courtyard of the prison of Berlin »Plötzensee«.

Tempered Krupp steel – you probably won't find a better blade »worldwide«. Just goes to show what German quality craftsmanship is.

The executioner and his aide step forward and look from on top into the half barrel – just as if this were the first severed head in their executioner's career.

"No. 2105, Karl-Heinz, a clean bit of work once again – and just look how he fell, his face looking nicely upward!"

"As always, Erich, we two are a good team – fast and painless – a lot better than that pedantic hanging!"

"And always lethal – precise – same spot every time."

Both henchmen are wearing strange looking masks, because despite of all the cruelty of their unusual office, they can't bring themselves to look the doomed man in the eyes, from »man to man«. In addition, they seem to be ashamed of what they are doing – a vocational occupation which is not credited by other people. Even with their peers, these two executors aren't all too poplar. And the Iron Cross, which they would so very much like to have, they probably won't get even at No. 3000.

To his children the executioner justifies and explains his work with the ever same tenor with the following words:

"Your father and his friend Erich have to do a very dangerous job every morning – for Fatherland and »Fuehrer«. Soon both of us will probably be awarded the Iron Cross, because it's about life and death each and every time!"

"… How strange, I, Eugen Wasner, can see the four eyes of my executioners – quite clearly now – even their pupils because both of them are bent over the barrel and are merely about 60 centimetres away from my head."

"This one was somehow different from all the others", begins the executioner,

"he actually lay down happily under that »thing« – look, Erich, how he is looking at us – just as if he were still alive – look at his eyes, his look is absolutely clear!"

"Well, yes, Hans, now don't frighten me! In the end you'll try to tell me that this fellow understands everything we are saying – even though he's dead as a doornail"

"Quite right, Erich, I can understand you, if that's the way you see it – this ghostly atmosphere – guillotine, six guards, hat grim looking court martial official as representative for the prosecution and the parson – and all that at 4:30 in the morning of a rainy day in November of 1943 – than your imagination isn't so farfetched. And then those two from the SS meticulously taking the minutes – we never had anything like that – the »Fuehrer« probably wants to know everything absolutely exactly in this case. Now, don't get melancholy, Erich, everything nothing but routine – nothing but No. 2105!"

"There, look!", the executioner goes on dumbfounded and actually gets quite excited – just as if he has just discovered something very important, and he bursts out:

"There! – Look! – A thick tear in his left eye!"

"Come now, that's from the rain."

"Nonsense, the whole of the killing machine is under a roof on eight metres high stilts, look up! There! – See! – There's a thick tear coming from his right eye, too! Look at it slowly getting bigger – quite clearly!"

"Really Karl –", and in his fright he even leaves out the second half of the double name.

"I, too, can see it mow. You are right! Blimey, that really is something! The fellow is crying and that even without a body!"

Now the executioner wants to see it exactly, for he has drawn a pair of glasses from his cape, which he puts over the slits in the mask. After a further short look, he turns away in fear and calls, while his voice sounds stifled and can only be heard in the immediate vicinity:

"Parson, Parson – do come here! Can you see it? The dead man is crying! The head is crying!"

The prison parson steps up to then, takes his hands from the pockets of his cape and beds over the barrel, leaning on its edge. He produces a small rectangular torchlight and shines the light into the open blue eyes of the executed.

"You see, gentlemen, Eugen Wasner has already met with the Lord – the severed head here, and then body there. The man is dead as dead can be, and his spirit has already met his Maker. But indeed, gentlemen, the face appears as if he were still alive. A content smile is recognizable, too, even though the pallor of death is, beyond doubt, on his countenance."

"… And this is where the parson is mistaken, because I, Eugen Wasner, am obviously not yet dead. I can see all three persons quite clearly – and I can hear them!"

Now all three of them rise, because the duty sergeant urges them to hurry up, and five people of a cleaning command are closing in on the double.

Three further offenders are waiting, so that the executioner and his henchman can once again fulfill their bloody trade. The executioner's bell is ringing again, too, calling the next in line!

"… And with me, the »**already dead Lance Corporal Wasner**« and the »**not yet dead Lance Corporal Wasner**« a very strange story is proceeding: The viewer of the entire scene could be very astonished, that a head parted from the body is still able to think, to see, to hear and even to cry!

Just like in a film, my whole life passes before me: Father, mother, the family – and I am feeling very close to my mother, so real, as if I still were inside her body – most heartfelt connected to her, protected, safe – nothing can happen to me – my mother is watching over me – and I, Eugen Wasner, feel secure on this earth!

Now the pictures of my childhood appear before me: The rural Leonding, we all speak in a wonderful dialect and are like one big family – the village school, the teachers, the class mates. Everything was so well-balanced until that day when »Adi« appeared.

In February of 1898[11] his family had moved to Leonding, and the father of »Adi« had taken up his new duties as a customs official on the border between Austria and Germany.

Yes, that »Adi«, I can see him quite clearly: Small, pale, black hair – but with a piercing look!

And »Adi« immediately livened up the game of the boys. Right from the beginning he wanted to be the leader whenever we player cops and robbers or Indians. »Adi« led the way and we ten others just always ran behind.

›That's the way it has to be! There must be one leader and the others have to follow!‹, and we thought that to be quite alright, because how were we to prevail in a battle against murderous Indians, if there wasn't one who would focus all of our power and the let the commando of ten attack as one.

And all of us were enthralled by »Adi«, because he did lead well – no matter if it were against the cruel Mongolians, the crafty Indians or the deceitful robbers.

›Every people needs a »Fuehrer«. Him you can then follow with confidence. Just as the leading stallion of a herd circumnavigates all dangers with talent, thus does the »Fuehrer« with the people!‹, that is what the then nine year old »Adi« already proclaimed.

Of course, we did follow our »General« without any contradiction. Clever talking along or even criticism – that »Adi« didn't like at all. Each and every decision had to be accepted without discussion, as if given by god. Even if only one of our team were to scrutinize anything, then »Adi« would scold – and when then his face turned red as a lobster and he foamed with anger, we would all be afraid of him!

---

[11] *Gustav Keller, Der Schüler Adolf Hitler – Die Geschichte eines lebenslangen Amoklaufs, publishing house Literatur Verlag Dr. W. Hopf, Berlin [2010], p. 21*

There was no necessity on our part to do a lot of thinking, and thus we soon followed »Adi« meekly – full of trust.

So we went from victory to victory. Even the deceitful Huns under King Attila trembled before the ingenious warlord »Adi« and had to retreat into their ancestral homelands in the East.

We eleven on our hobby-horses, with self made swords, bows and arrows, made the army of horse riders with their 100,000 broke-down nags tremble. Thanks to our brilliant warlord »Adi« there were no enemies under God's heavens that we would have to fear. Such games really were fun, and nobody thought of school or homework anymore. It was like a drug with an unrestrained hunger for more.

Always of special importance was our messenger on horseback who had to convey »Adi's« orders from Army Group A to Army Group B. How a messenger can get unhindered through enemy territory »Adi« showed us, his comrades, again and again. He demonstrated it repeatedly.

›The messenger‹, he used to say,

›is actually the most important soldier immediately after the warlord. Because, if the messenger fails, the order of the supreme command will not arrive where it belongs. Chaos will ensue! The battle is lost!

Victories are all that count!‹, »Adi« instructed us again and again.

And all ten of us were literally drunk from everything »Adi« drummed into us day by day – what better is there than success! To us, »Adi's« word was like law, and soon we all were absolutely convinced, too, that only discipline and obedience led to the success of every warrior.

Then there was »Fat Erwin« who simply because of the mass of his body had been our leader before. »Adi« made it clear to us and to Erwin, too, that fatness and strength were no prerequisite to make you a born leader, but only intelligence together with an iron will.

But »Fat Erwin« hadn't quite understood the »new times«. His little bit of brain obviously hadn't grown to the same extent as his rotund »pig's head«, as »Adi« called it.

»Fat Erwin« stirred up wherever he could, and tried to split off a couple of warriors of the eleven we were originally, and »Adi« said:

›Erwin, you are my friend, and the best fighter of my forces. But you must learn to obey orders – and I am the »Fuehrer«. Otherwise you will weaken our »army«. We must stick together to the death!‹

And we shouted

›Our »Fuehrer«, may he live!‹

So it happened as it had to: »Fat Erwin« kept on stirring, and his little brain in that oversized head really hadn't understood that friendly warning.

So then one day, »Fat Erwin« ran to his father and mother and screaming loudly, having been beaten black and blue by »Adi's« raiding party.

Fortunately the hay harvest was on, and Erwin's father was a burly farmer with a square head, but who amazingly immediately struck the right note:

›Here Erwin, here's a pitch fork, and there, Erwin‹,

and the farmer pointed to the hay with his calloused hands and repeated:

›there, Erwin, that hay there is your bad Indians – and now »fight«!‹

»Fat Erwin's« mother had overheard everything, came up to them, and the young, chubby woman wasn't at all angry at her son's companions.

›Come, Erwin, have a nice slice of bread‹, and she handed him a slice of bread with sausage.

»Fat Erwin« ate, drank a lemonade – spit in his hands – and full of energy really got into that hay!

After that we were no longer eleven, but only ten of us, but the grouch was gone – like dead – forever!"

… And in fractions of seconds his thoughts literally speed though his brain – the brain in the severed head of Eugen Wasner – the head of the lance corporal of the German »Wehrmacht« – the head now lying in a round barrel under the guillotine, and whose blue eyes are staring motionlessly upward!

And the brain of the head is still capable of arranging thoughts and to summarize these thoughts to a story of days long gone by:

"I can quite clearly see the first day of the holidays. As agreed, we met by the little forest – and our group was there over- punctually, with coats of mail, swords and other weapons. Secretly we were tense with expectation of what »Adi« had planned.

We knew that at this time, there was big trouble between »Adi« and his father. The customs official once again hadn't held back – only his mother had saved her son from a bleeding bottom. Fearlessly she went between her brutal husband and the child of nine years. Two blows of the cane she bravely caught on her own body.

Completely incomprehensible for »Adi« what was happening there: His father, tending to outbursts of rage, had found it necessary to give him a threshing, only because his mark in mathematics had, compared with the previous year, gone down one step.

Now »Adi«, too, arrived, armed with spear, round shield and leather helmet. The thin legs covered with adhesive tape and bandages – his »old man« had really slammed into him, and we pitied him, the way he came along everything but a leader – dragging one leg a bit.

It was absolutely clear to »Adi«, that the mighty hiding had done damage to his reputation, because his cries of pain and the yells of rage of the official could be heard for miles. And »Adi« was ashamed of himself – not because of the bad mark in mathematics – no, because of his helplessness from his brutal father. Only the cries of his brave mother ended this terrible scene – and really and truly:

The new heroine of the village was Clara Hitler!

›Let's go, children‹, »Adi« immediately began, and all nine of us listened to what was to come. And »Adi« surprised us all with his idea. It had to be something »fantastic«, so as to make up for and distract from the shock to his leading position caused by the degrading punishment by his father, in which he had clearly been the loser.

›Listen, men, we want to start off into the holidays with a really big bang!‹, and we were listening all tense to what »Adi« had thought up.

›Men‹, he started anew, after we had all sat down in a circle. »Adi« was sitting slightly higher up on a tree stump. Our weapons we had neatly arranged in front of us, just as »Adi« had always demanded of us.

I, Eugen Wasner, was sitting to the right, and Bruno Kneisel to the left of »Adi« – we were the sub-chiefs. Thus we performed the beginning of our holidays on the clearing on the moss under the venerable fir trees. We called this small hill our »discussion thingstead« – but the discussion went as always: »Adi« lectured!

›Men, soldiers, my warriors‹, he went on again, and the tension grew. What is »Adi« up to this time? And we turned all red in the face because of all the uncertainty that tormented us.

›Men, soldiers, my undaunted warriors – dear friends.‹

›Looks like we're in for some fun and games‹, I thought,

›he's got something in mind with us, »Adi« doesn't call us »dear friends« for nothing.‹

Now there followed a pause – a long pause – and »Adi« knew, that this creates tension in his audience so that unquenched curiosity and impatience can nearly painfully be felt.

… And suddenly I, Eugen Wasner, can see the coming events outsized – and by no means like a story from a far gone past. The action from already 45 years ago seizes me with such reality, as if everything is happening at this moment and not in former times – and I, the inconspicuous Eugen, am in it – one of the protagonists:

›Friends, it is to be a test of courage with which we will honorably begin our holidays as warriors‹, »Adi« blows the gaff.

The nine of us are sitting with open mouths, literally hanging on every word of our spokesman – our breath nearly falters.

**›Men, who would be daring enough
to piddle a billy goat into its mouth?‹**

The nine of us laugh a bit – more artificially and from embarrassment – because the surprise effect is so overwhelming that we really don't know what else we could have done.

Again the tension rises. None of us is capable of moving – we just sit there, motionless, gaping.

›Who dares, men?‹, »Adi« repeats, and involuntarily we reach for our »pee-pees« as protection against the sharp teeth of the billy goat. In our minds, blood is already gushing everywhere. All of us it runs cold down our spines. Horrified we think of the terrible mouth of the »monster«.

›But »Adi« ‹, sub-chief Bruno Kneisel takes the word, an all of us aren't sure if this won't trigger one of »Adi's« fits of rage, because the »but Adi« is already something like an intervention to the idea of the test of courage.

But to the surprise of all of us, »Adi« is absolutely tame – doesn't go about shouting – but take up the word quite friendly and really brotherly amiable:

›I will do it myself, if none of you dare!‹ he says, and we all look at him in awe and with eyes wide open.

›That is a »Fuehrer«! ‹, we think and literally idolize our »Adi«.

›He is brave, so entirely different to us fearful ones from the »lower ranks«!‹

›But »Adi« ‹ sub chief Bruno Kneisel dares once again,

›Your ideas are always great, but this time you are going too far. Up to now we have only been playing the stories of Karl May and others, and it was always very funny. We weren't scarping the barrel then – but now it gets as hard as nails – you can't really be serious about us piddling into the beast's mouth. That is pure horror , and I'm, to be honest, really afraid – and I fear for you, too.‹

We all need a break, not only Bruno Kneisel after his long speech. A little hope arises in us that »Adi« may abandon his insane plan. He too keeps to the break, seeming very much introverted, staring pensively at his weapons in front of him. But then suddenly, without any warning, he jumps up, points with arm and index finger out of the thingstead, obviously in the direction where he suspects the bill goat to be, and shouts in his high child's voice:

›I'll do it! I'm going to piddle the animal into its huge mouth! And here's a bet: Each of you will give me a bar of chocolate if I do it, and I'll give each one of you two bars of chocolate if I don't do it. Your hands on it and you're on, and I have to save up for a whole year if my courage fails me!‹

The nine of us look at each other. From experience we know, that now »Adi« won't tolerate any contradiction – his decision is already final! And because we don't even as much as try to change his mind, there is from nine mouths a chorus as one:

›You're on!‹

›Come, let's go to the meadow, there's a billy goat there!‹, our »Fuehrer« orders, and all of us trundle along behind.

AND THERE IT IS!

White, gigantically huge and with enormous horns he grabs grass with is more than large mouth, tears off the blades of grass with his lower front teeth and chews the juicy grass with his molars which are further back in his mouth.

While the nine of us are still standing at the fence undecided, »Adi« already slips through the middle wires. Meanwhile the billy goat is looking in our direction, still voluptuously crushing the green grass.

›The eyes of the billy goat are somewhat deep red and the entire face appears dangerous. A really sly and shifty »fellow«, that he-goat‹, I am still in thought while »Adi« has already gone right up to the oversized animal. He holds green leaves before its mouth which the billy goat obviously accepts gladly – tears them with its lower incisors to then chew them up.

›If only he knew what »Adi« is up to !‹, it races through my brain.

›Would the billy goat still be standing there so coolly, taking the grass from »Adi's« hands? Quite familiar with one another they seem – the human and the animal, too!‹

›Come along, you heroes‹, »Adi« calls out to us impatiently. And we, too, give the creature – appearing to us so threatening – something to eat. Dandelions we have plucked, and the billy goat really eats noisily and is obviously happy about the tasty and unexpected meal.

Then everything happens really fast:
- I hold the billy goat by its buttocks with my strong arms, his thighs clamped between my legs.
- Bruno Kneisel pries open the mouth of the billy goat and pushes a stick between its upper and lower jaws.
- The billy goat grunts a bit, most likely from pain, because the stick drills itself into his sensitive mouth.

But the billy goat doesn't move, has been taken too much by surprise by the sudden action of Bruno Kneisel and me – everything happens so fast, that for the two of us there isn't even time to be afraid.

- »Adi« drops his pants, pulls up his shirt and holds the ends by his teeth.
- His back bent backwards and his belly stuck out in front, he places his »zippedeus« immediately on the lips of the animal and begins to piddle.
- »Adi« is piddling and the urine is running out of the billy goat's mouth.

›See‹, says »Adi«,

›it's quite easy‹, pushes his lower body still a bit further forward and lays his »zippedeus« on the lower lip of the billy goat.

To even more enjoy his courage, »Adi« raises his arms and piddles »no hands«.

THEN IT HAPPENS!

- The billy goat snaps shut!
- The lower teeth, sharp as knives, dig into »Adi's« »pee-pee« and press it against the upper bone plate, because Bruno Kneisel had suddenly pulled the stick from the terrible mouth.
- Blood gushes from the billy goat's mouth – »Adi«" yells out –

›Ouch, help!‹ loud and shrilly, screaming with pain!

Probably because of the strident cry on that meadow of Leonding in the year 1898, the billy goat for a second opens its mouth. – »Adi« is released!

The shirt falls from his mouth. Drawing up his pants with his left hand and holding the other protective before his pee-pee, he races off like a hurricane shouting and screaming – most likely a savage pain at the most sensitive spot of the body of a nine years old boy.

We »remaining« nine are as paralyzed with fright, – incapable of uttering even just one word. Only the billy goat seems totally unmoved, tears up the grass once more with his front teeth, only to go on voluptuously chew it up in the back part of its mouth.

We remaining nine of this mean children's prank look at each other with eyes wide open, and the same question arises in all of us:

›Has this insidious, evil billy goat bitten off, chewed up and even swallowed »Adi's« »zippedeus«?‹

46

We nine »comrades-in arms« of this macabre game have never got an answer. The billy goat and »Adi«, too, kept their secret to themselves and never did they reveal it!

Next day all nine of us had to completely appear before the customs official, »Adi's« father: Under threat of daily thrashings with a two-metre-long cane we had to swear by the Lord, never to talk about this story. Father, mother, siblings, and relatives of »Adi« weren't to be talked about because of a silly prank of their son – with extremely painful injuries to a part of a »man« which one simply doesn't talk about!

I, Lance Corporal Eugen Wasner, am probably the only one who has broken the vow.

Is that one of the reasons why I now have to die? In the prime of my life I must leave this earth, the once so beautiful earth, now soaked with the blood of millions of innocents – men, women, little children – damned war!

Now once more the executioner's bell rings in my ear on my severed head in the barrel under the guillotine, 1943, in the yard of the prison Berlin-Plötzensee. The bell is calling the next doomed candidate!

I feel how my senses are fading, the rest of my blood leaving my brain and running warm along my neck into the wooden barrel. The last pictures of the »film of my life« are already becoming blurred – are becoming indistinct, and I am happy. My path on earth is ending – and it ends for a story which is true. Or is the path ending because of the vow I have broken to »Adi's« father?

It is getting dark, and I am being carried by a dear person – by my so dearly beloved mother. She holds me in her arms in my full length – whole once again with head and body!

And my mother is smiling, and I am smiling, too,

and the load my other has to carry is not heavy, I am so very light, feeling light as a feather,

carried by earthly love over to the love of God – soon I will be standing before my creator!"

The last images become blurred to indistinctness:
- The »Film of Life« of Eugen Wasner ends.
- And so ends his life on earth, too!

Trials and Tribulations –
The 2.5 million lightyears distant »Toranians« solve the secret of incarnation

….. "I, Immo, feel to be even smaller than I already am – two million light years distant from the macabre scene in the inner courtyard of the prison in Berlin-Plötzensee in the year 1943.

›Tell me, father, how is it possible for a cut-off head to live on?‹

And father and I see on our huge plasma screen the next offender being taken to the place of execution – in this case dragged across the ground by the escort commando. The sentenced man is obviously not yet ready to die.

›Yes, my son, with humans it is so, that the pictures of their lives still go through their minds, even though they have, by their own judgment and medical knowledge, already been pronounced »dead«. They can then still feel – even cry, as you, my son, have just seen. Persons who have been »seemingly dead« have often told about this »film of their life« after awakening and returning to this life.

We, on the other hand, on »Tora« cannot feel like humans – **happiness, sorrow, joy** are perceptions that were already lost to us many millions of years ago. It is simply because all the functions of our body are controlled by chips situated in our heads. We are not even able to cry. We are thus in the actual sense, nothing but machines, even though we resemble humans in a lot of ways.

Moreover, in the course of our lives, for which we may well be granted 70,000 or 80,000 years, all organs and limbs are replaced several times – and when the »switch« is turned on death, we are really dead – and that instantly!

Pity actually, we »Toranians«, too, would really love to have feelings like humans and also like the »Keranians«. Our existence would be much more endearing. But those are merely dreams, pious hopes. Unfortunately we can never regain the ability of emotion – despite our more than enormous intelligence. In that, the primitive creatures on Earth I and Earth II are vastly superior to us.

We »Toranians«, too, were once long, long times ago, capable of beautiful emotions like

- being happy
- being cheerful

- being sad

and also, of being glad about something.

It all began, when about 65 million years ago, the dinosaurs became extinct on Earth. A comet from outer space destroyed the lives of all the large animals and plants, too. Storms, fire blazes and floods raced over the globe and eliminated nearly all life on Earth I. But, as it is on a small scale it is also on a big one: New life rises from the ashes of the scorched earth!

Ad now be amazed, my son‹, my father goes on,

›the result of what came forth from the wrecked earth of those days, in the beginning only hesitantly and weak, is what you see here today on our planet »Tora«:

Our intelligent people, that had its origin in that devastated planet Earth!

Yes, it is actually one of our greatest secrets:

We »Toranians« stem from the Earth of the Humans!

We developed quickly – just as the animals and flora did.

Yes, my son, we »Toranians« are the ancestors of the Humans, which, of course, they don't know and not imagine even in the slightest. Even if they read this novel they will not believe it, though grappling with the thought of their origin from times immemorial – because they know that something about their origin is still in the dark!

Some are of the opinion, that humans are descendant from monkeys. Others follow the opinion that becoming human developed from a different line of descent – developed from microbes to small living organisms and to the learning of the upright walk and on to Homo sapiens.

A third theory to becoming human claims that everything is to be attributed to a god, a creator. So you can read it in the great book hey call the Bible:

»God sent Adam and Eve, so that they might reproduce!«

In this group, science is not so much in demand. Instead, their belief sets in. It always happens, my son, when humans do not have a proper explanation, like for instance, for their descent, life in general, mortality and life after death.

One could certify all three theoretical directions, that their advocates in the question of evolution into man are not so far wrong. There is a bit of truth in all three of these directions of thought. They are, in some way, on the right track – suspecting the goal, but remaining nebulously because of a final, missing confirmation.

It is astonishing, with which energy and intensity mankind is looking for practicable explanations concerning his descent; virtually with dogged determination to find answers to that question.

So now you will once again be astonished at my explaining a few things to you which you haven't yet worked on in the course of your studies:

We »Toranians« have developed at a rapid speed after that terrible disaster on the Earth of the Humans more than 65 million years ago.

You can compare our fast increase in performance in knowledge and development by all means with that of Humans and »Keranians«. Only these species are, with their merely 200,000 years of history of development, still very young, so that their intelligence has not yet reached the stage of ours.

So we were soon capable of visiting other stars, planets and solar systems. During the history of our evolution we managed forthwith to reach travelling speeds in space which corresponded to a multiple of the speed of light[12]. Soon it was no problem for us to travel at speeds above one billion of kilometers per second.

Hereto small comparisons of illustration as to the enormously high speed of travel: Beside metre and kilometre we have introduced as a new measure of length, the circumference of Earth I[13].

Thereby an auxiliary dimension was created so that even human thinking could get a small impression of the vast distances in space: A space ship at the speed of light would thus circumnavigate the equator 7.5 times per second.

---

[12] *The speed of light is about 300,000 kilometres per second.*

[13] *The circumference of the Earth of Humans, measured at the equator is about 40,000 kilometres.*

At a speed of a billion kilometres per second the number of laps around the equator would rise to 25,000 – going at 3375 times the speed of light.

At this speed we reached our new home on »Tora« in the Andromeda Galaxy after about 600 years of the Humans – an in those, by all means, days adequate time of travel. Because our life expectancy had risen to many thousands of years, there was no problem as to this question.

Even the distance to »Tora« was, because of the nearly infinite distance of on 2 million light years, not to be achieved with normally fuelled flight objects – be it diesel, kerosene or nuclear fission.

So today our space ships carry only the amount of fuel necessary to sustain for about 600 years of flight, all needs of the crew and internal technical systems.

On the outside of the ships there is nothing – solely a smooth surface.

To our assistance there came a huge step in our history of evolution without which unencumbered and fast travel in space would not be possible.

We achieved to tame the largest known energy in space and to utilize it for space travel:

»Black Holes«!

»Black Holes« can be used to destroy or create whole stars and planets. Thus no other power in space could challenge us, should a warlike conflict arise. The danger of an intergalactic war has thus been banished for all times. Wars will only occur between underdeveloped species, Humans, »Keranians«, »Kerstakians« on their Earths I, II, and III.

If we wanted, for instance, travel from »Tora« to the Earth of the Humans, we would prepare a space tunnel for the whole trip of 2 million light years. This flight channel is then also cleared of all other straying objects, so that the actual path of travel is free of unwanted obstacles.

Our space ship has got the ideal shape for flight – that is to say that of a sphere:

robust,

sturdy and equipped with

the largest possible volume in connection with the smallest hull!

The energy of the »Black Hole« is thus applied, that the spherical ship is not only drawn through the tunnel, but at the same time pushed from behind. The enormous forces acting on the bodies of the crew during acceleration and deceleration, too, shall not be investigated here – that is a problem which we had already solved a long time ago.

Humans and »Keranians« as well, are constantly surprised at not making any progress in space travelling despite continuously racking their brains. The cause is simply that, referring to the »boundlessness of space«, the small human and »Keranian« brains are not in any way suited to work out sustainable solutions in a comprehensible way. We »Toranians«, too, were in need of an entirely new intellectual approach as well as the development of new languages and mathematical operations – which only machines could handle.

Even if the ingenious physicist Albert Einstein from the Earth of the Humans had had further 10,000 »Einsteins« to his assistance, his space ship, travelling at speeds possible today, would not be able to even reach the first star in his own solar system (5 light years ≈ 50 trillion kilometres). For them, the intergalactic dream of mankind could, in these days, never come true!

A TV programme by the name of »Star Trek« has already realized that one would have to travel at a speed of at least one billion kilometres per second to reach other worlds. The engineers of »Star Trek« for instance subdivide their speeds from »Warp 1« to »Warp 15«.

These »Warp stages« are raised to the power of three and then multiplied by the speed of light.

For »Warp 2« for instance, this means:

    2^3 x 300,000 kilometres per second

=   8 x 300,000 kilometres per second

=   2,400,000 kilometres per second.

For »Warp 15« it means:

    15^3 x 300,000 kilometres per second

=   3375 x 300,000 kilometres per second

=   1,000,000,000 (1 billion) kilometres per second.

In words: At »Warp 15« you travel at a speed of 1 billion kilometres per second through space.

In the aforesaid film, humans do fly rather fast and far, knowing that their propulsion energy is stored inside the space ship in the form of fuel.

The question remains: How far do they really think they will get, once they have left their dream factory »film«?

If in the end their space ship were as big as that of the »Toranians« – even with a spherical shape of 10 kilometres in diameter and thus 523 cubic metres of room for fuel tanks – the journey would, because of the almost infinite distances, quickly be at an end!

Consider, that just the flight distance from the Earth of the Humans to »Tora« corresponds to about 10 trillion[14] kilometres multiplied by 2 million years of flight.

In numbers it means:

10,000,000,000,000 x 2,000,000

= 20,000,000,000,000,000,000 kilometres

= 20 quintillion kilometers.

As this problem is well known to science on the Earth of the Humans, and one knows that the amount of fuel possible in the space ship is absolutely tiny compared to the aspired, huge distances in the »boundlessness of space«, some have constructed themselves a mnemonic.

One doesn't fly 2,000,000 light years from A to B (Illus. 3, top, page 54), no, one just folds up the whole of space like a sheet of paper – in the extreme case one half sheet directly on the other half sheet, and only passes through the sheets (Illus. 3 bottom, page 54).The satiric would say: »Solved simply ingeniously!«

---

[14] *1 light year is the equivalent of about 10 trillion kilometers – thus calculated:*

1 year in seconds
365 days x 24 hours x 60 minutes x 60 seconds
≈ 31,000,000 seconds

1 light year in kilometres
31,000,000 seconds x 300,000 kilometres per second
≈ 10,000,000,000,000 kilometres (10 x 10^{12} kilometres)
= 1 trillion kilometres (confirm my calculation, if you will)

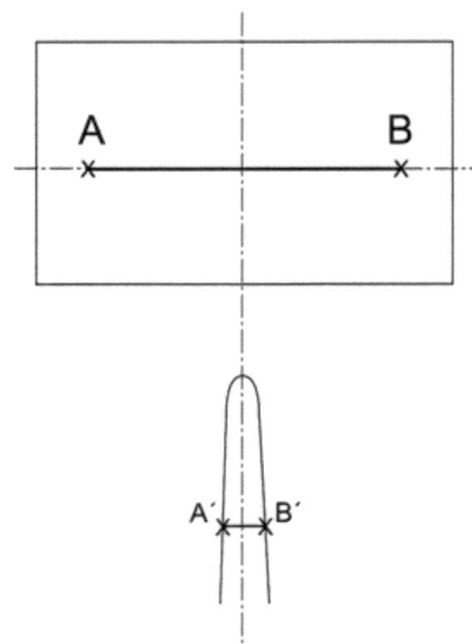

Illus. 3 Diagram – »Space« folded like a sheet of paper: The path from A to B is substantially reduced to the distance A' to B'.

Recently there was a TV program[15] on the Earth of the Humans, in which it showed that one had come quite close to the solution of the descent of humans.

Scientists had recognized, that within the limitations of their genetic reflections, all people on Earth I are descendant from the same ancestors. Even the late President Mobuto of the Congo had adopted these new findings, proclaiming in reference to all humans on this planet, the following:

›We are all one big family, because we all have the same ancestors!‹

Considered seriously in the actual sense, there are no Chinese, Japanese, Europeans, Mongolians, Arabs, Indians or Africans – The genes prove it: We all have the same »forefather«!

The genes, the genetic make-up of all peoples, is the same in its origin, no matter if they be yellow, black, white or even red.

According to that, about 70,000 years ago there was in Africa a small group of about 10,000 individuals[16]. The species then immigrated in parts into Asia, Australia, Europe and via Alaska to America.

The originally black skinned people adapted relatively quickly to the climate in their new environments, and developed in their

---

[15] *»A Question of Genes: Is the human race one big family?« ARTE, theme night on October 18th of 2011*

[16] *ibidem*

evolutionary adaption to the new surroundings different colours of skin like white, yellow, brown or red, too.

The essence of these findings:

>>The cradle of the human race stands in Africa<<.

Now, my son, you could say: If the humans should manage to overcome themselves, then it is only a small step to the truth. They complement the statement in their >>Bible<<:

>>**God sent Adam and Eve as first humans to Earth**<<, says the Bible and we >>Toranians<< add >>**and he sent them to Africa and their skin was black!**<<

Then, of course, the afore mentioned President Mobuto is right in saying:

>>The cradle of the human race stands in Africa – with the same mother and father as ancestors.<<

This means that on this Earth aren't any separate peoples, but that we are really one big family in which, at the beginning, everyone had the same genetic make-up! And indeed, my son, in this aspect the humans have nearly solved the question of their descent – nearly, I must add, because the essential is still missing!

In order for you, my son, to make progress in your studies of history, I still have to give you some more pieces of information.

When we >>Toranians<<, after a few millions of years, had reached the stage of intelligence to rule space, it was high time to also use these, our abilities,
because:

- There was mismanagement on Earth, compared to what humans will achieve if they keep going the way they are now.

- Nuclear fuel rods and all the other garbage of the technical society we had stored beneath us in the interior of the Earth, in the oceans and in the atmosphere.

- The little sphere was downright bled dry, yes, literally sucked out, because everything useful, like hot vapors, lava, and all natural resourced, we had taken out.

- As compensation for the upkeep of the equilibrium all accumulated poisons like carbon monoxide, carbon dioxide, sulphorous vapors etc. were pumped into the interior of the Earth.

Since, without planning, we took everything that industrial nations need from favourable places, and gave back to the Earth our poisonous refuse, without planning, in other places, the result was:

The small globe with its just on 12,000 kilometres in diameter became instable!

The »sphere« looked just like an old football from which the air had escaped – a football so ugly and useless than not one child would have wanted to »play« with it!

Huge fissures under the oceans – tsunamis – green house effect with the melting of the poles – rise of sea level resulting in the sinking of whole cities, countries and continents – wars with conventional and nuclear weapons: Small countries threw nuclear bombs on small neighbouring countries, with the result that radioactive clouds hit big countries, too – daily reports of horror of flooding alternating with periods of drought – forests one could only view in documentary films – revolutions »worldwide« and he young generations rebelled, too – the population grew unrestrained – the fight for work, water, bread and money escalated – nobody would wait any more, patience became a word unknown – the »non-owning« took what they needed from those that »owned« which could only be achieved if the head was cut off as well – the struggle over distribution between the single peoples became absolutely murderous, and animal killed animal, too, if their own young were starving – diseases arose out of the blue and like from nowhere, not only taking the lives of millions, but of billions!

We had »made« it:
The »small sphere» was completely going wild!

But then something utterly unexpected happened.

The really last remaining part of the human population united, focused all their energy and knowledge with only one goal:

Immigration to »Tora« in the Andromeda Galaxy!

That was for us the last remaining opportunity, because a series of ice ages announced themselves at very high speed.

Thus it came, my son, that the remaining last of once **twenty-five billion** inhabitants of the Earth fled before themselves and the ice ages! When we had settled in on our new home planet »Tora«, which we called Earth IV, we were ready to learn from our history – from the failure of whole peoples.

After we had overcome the »human way of thinking« on »Tora«, life – and economy models were developed by our huge computer centres and »computer brains« which considered each one of us as »equal individual« among »equals«:

- Rich and poor
- Hunger and abundance
- Infirmity and illness
- Masters and slaves.

All that did not exist anymore with us.

With the elimination of »human egoism« a new era began for all of us!

All you still see today, my son, in the actions of the »Star Trek« films on Earth I is, of course, only a »fantastic tissue of imagination« of the humans there.

Just like the humans of today are polarized, after all, is the way they think of intergalactic life outside their solar system.

Whenever their space ships reach far distant worlds, there is immediately again

- Envy
- Hatred
- Suppression
- Striving for power to the extent of world domination.

All to be summarized under the generic term:
»EGOISM«.

Creatures that one encounters on intergalactic journeys can only be evil, deceitful, treacherous and domineering!

Because this is imprinted on the way of thinking of humans, encounters with extraterrestrial life must always lead to violence using thrust-, cutting-, fire- and laser arms.

The »Star Trek« films show this way of thought which dominates, like a law, the cinematic processing of fictitious events in interstellar space.

Because humans and »Keranians« have so far been incapable of learning, other than we »Toranians« have , from their own history, we wanted to find out if this were an unwritten law, valid for all times.

Thus, in those days on »Tora« we had decided the following:

We wanted to carry out a large-scale experiment:

We wanted to determine, if a race like ours will go through the same stages of development if confronted with the same conditions that we found on Earth I in those days.

And now be amazed, my son:

For this purpose we actually placed two human individuals on the then empty Earth I, 200,000 years ago in Africa, who were more or less genetically identical with the »Homo Sapiens« of today – a young man and a young woman with jet-black colour of skin! In contrast to other life forms, they were equipped with intelligence and a physique which, in a wider sense, allowed them to walk upright and to produce primitive tools for the acquisition of nourishment.

By that, the great book of humans, the »Bible«, is in parts confirmed. What they had written in this book since the birth of Christ – apart from descent from God and colour of skin – is true:

**The black Adam and the black Eve really are
the »forefather« and »first mother« of mankind!**

From then on, many universities on »Tora« pursued, how from a black couple of humans, let's actually call them that, how these two people developed to become the seven billion people of the 21st Century on Earth I – white, yellow, brown, red and black as well!

The goal that we had set ourselves for this large-scale experiment was: Find out, if the species »Humans« developed exactly like we »Toranians«.

- Will the species »Humans« possibly learn from their own history, so that mistakes made once will not repeat?
- Will they possibly learn faster than we did or will they, to the contrary maneuver themselves even faster into the abyss of a self-destructive apocalypse of this small globe?

Those are the questions not only of historical interest to us, but also to use the conclusions discovered, to prevent us from possibly making wrong decisions in the future. We neither are immune to making mistakes of far-reaching consequences for our further life.

As we found similar conditions on Earth II as on Earth I, the same large-scale experiment was carried out there. We called the new inhabitants »Keranians«.

With that, there were two large-scale experiments being carried out on two similar planets, light years apart. The experiments having started simultaneously, there were always opportunities for comparison with the help of supervisons:

Two couples of jet-black skin were the beginning of everything, and filled our people with a nearly unrestrained interest to find out what would become of the two beautiful girls and the two handsome youths – we can see an interim result today in the year 2012 after the calendar on Earth I, the Earth of the Humans.

So to make absolutely sure, that the long- term experiments on the »Earth of the Humans« and on the »Earth of the Keranians« could be carried out totally autonomous and without any influence from the outside, already in the preamble of our constitution has been set:

›[…] Any further development of humans and of »Keranians«, too, has to take place without any influence of the »Toranians«. Intervention into the issues concerning the there present peoples by the »Toranians« is impossible. Even in the case of events like inventions, large building endeavors, wars, diseases, acts of murder and other cruelties there will be no help or intervention by the »Toranians«.

The main university on »Tora« will accompany both long-term experiments on a scientific basis, will coordinate all efforts of other universities aiming in the same direction, and will thoroughly report to the people of »Tora« on an annual basis.

Every inhabitant on »Tora« is thus linked via huge computers to the other two Earths, that every adult, but every child as well, can follow the events there in detail – supersized plasma TV screens on »Tora« allow the surveillance of each and even the smallest of actions.‹

You will surely ask yourself, my son, if there aren't any traces left of us »Toranians« after our »brief appearance« of many millions of years on the Earth of the Humans.

Indeed, small and large ice ages have changed the surface of the Earth to the extent that practically nothing reminds of us. After us, new land masses, mountain ranges, oceans and even entire continents were formed in other places. And yet, a find on the

Earth of the Humans some two or three years ago, let us prick our ears:

A small, humanoid figurine enclosed in amber was found – dated to an age of several millions of years!

›Were there actually »humanlike creatures« on Earth I, millions of years old?‹ – was the question of science.

Of course, there were – I can give the answer, my son – only it isn't the effigy of an »early ancestor« of mankind, considering the lines of development of their family tree, but that of a »Toranian«.

But, if you wish, is the figurine found in amber at the same time the portrayal of an early ancestor of mankind, because they had been taken to the Earth by the »Toranians« as their descendants.

There is, even with humans, the theory that organic life didn't stem from the Earth, but could have come »**flying**« from space – no matter if in the form of a microbe or any other form of life.

So we »Toranians« do have to smile a bit on hearing the just explained. In this case both is, of course, true:

- The »Toranians« developed from the materials of their former home planet Earth I. Thus the humans of today are to be considered to indirectly be descendants of the »Toranians« and also a product of the materials mentioned and of the same Earth.
- But mankind did come »flying« from space to Earth – but in this case not in the form of microbes, but already »complete« as black Adam and his wife, black Eve!

Thus, my son, sometimes both is wrong, but sometimes both is right, too.‹

›That was a very interesting and educational history lesson, indeed‹, I, Immo as the son, thank my father.

It will be seen, to what extent the historic development of the »Toranians« Humans and »Keranians« will help me to understand the further circumstances and doings of the »Fuehrer« Adolf Hitler and to rate them in a larger context.

›Will I possibly be able to better work on the task put to myself, after having heard such a lot about the origin and evolution of the Humans and also about their dependence on us »Toranians« ‹, I ask myself and am, in view of the task before me, very confident."

…..

»Vienna Stories« of a Youth –
Adolf Hitler at the age of 17/18 in his mind already »Fuehrer« of the world

Illus. 4   Drawing –
Hitler at the age of sixteen

– the only known portrayal
from his youth.

On the 21st of November of 1908, the music student August Kubizek hurries towards Stumpergasse of the City of Vienna. There, at Number 29, Door 17 on the second floor, with the old lady Aneliese Zakreys in the Vienna district Mariahilf, he had left his friend »Adi« – full name Adolf Hitler – behind.

He, »Gustl« as he was called in friendship by »Adi«, has just returned from an alternative community service practice in Linz. Now he is glad to be back in Vienna and is absolutely happy to see »Adi« again – his only friend.

"But why am I so anxious? What is tormenting me? Why am I so afraid of the reunion? »Adi« had written only a few days ago, that he is well and that he is happy to see me."

Still the whole joy of reunion is shadowed by uncertainty:

"How did my friend get along with the solitude, all that time without me? Will he really be happy when, after such a long time, we will look each other in the eyes again? Most certainly we will embrace, like real men, heartily squeeze one another, with a kiss on the cheek – just like is the custom here with us. But, oh my God, »Adi« isn't there anymore, simply moved out!

›But Mrs. Zakreys‹, I ask our landlady, flabbergasted.

›Where then has he gone to? – For God's sake, hasn't he left any kind of message for me?‹

›No, Mr. Kubizek‹, and she lowers her look to the floor, just as if it was partly her fault, and now she raises her eyes, now looking me in the face.

›Mr. Hitler has paid his part of the rent on November the 18th, stowed away into his suitcase all his many books along with his picture folders, and off he went!‹

Now that is a shock – a harsh disappointment in my so young life of merely twenty years! My best friend has gone, simply disappeared the slightest »peep«.

Very obvious:

-   This is the break off of our friendship.
-   That is its end!

Why on earth did »Adi« choose this painful way?

No regards, no farewell, no thanks for the time spent together, no adieus!

»Adi«, too, is already 19 years old, only nine months younger than I am – he should actually know, that such is not proper – he who has always valued etiquette and manners so much – totally incomprehensible the whole event!

Anyone who sees me now will ask,

›What is the matter with August Kubizek?‹

I would actually like to scream my sorrow into the face of anyone walking by:

›My friend, my only friend, has left me – a friendship that had grown over years simply broken off abruptly – what a punch below the belt!‹

No wonder that people throw me pitying glances – strangers walking by.

Czechs, Hungarians, Austrians, Germans and Jews, too, roam around in Vienna in the year 1908 – all in all twelve different nations with considerably differing religions. Vienna is, with its 2,000,000 inhabitants, the sixth largest city on Earth, a colourful mixture from all provinces of the Austro-Hungarian Empire.

But I, Alfred Kubizek, don't take notice of any of them, those so strange faces in a bubbling metropolis – I can only see one single person – myself.

But why has my friend »Adi« chosen this way? Why couldn't he, who is so clever, have thought of some different possibility for a parting of friends?

Why this way? – And my heart aches with all that sorrow.

»Adi« and I have been through so much!

What reasons could a friend have, choosing to draw a line so painful for the friend?

What haven't we been through – pleasant and unpleasant. And we did understand each other so well, actually the ideal pair of friends:

- »Adi« so very convincing and determined
- I the more willing listener, deeply taking his stories in.

Somehow we complemented one another ideally, a friendship that worked, even though two entirely different characters meeting each other.

»Adi« was for me, from the beginning, likeable – he did and thought everything so differently from me, that little decorator's apprentice.

»Adi« wanted to become an artist, and for that he didn't even need a »bread-and-butter job«, like the one a decorator does have to carry out. Good heavens, was that an amazing person – my friend »Adi« – a »bread-and-butter job«, an entirely new term that I hadn't even heard of before.

And how well-read »Adi« was, running to the library every day and buying the news papers. He was absolutely interested in every subject. A young man eager to learn, who, already as an adolescent, stored and filtered every bit of reachable knowledge thus that it fitted to his already preconceived overall opinion.

›But what was this »overall opinion«?‹ I'm asking myself today, sitting in a teeming crowd in the Vienna of the 1908s.

The functioning of our friendship was actually based on a very simple principle – that is becoming clear to me while I am sitting here – sitting here all alone, without »Adi« pestering me with his fits of rage.

No matter what it was about, I wasn't only to listen – quiet as a mouse – I did have to applaud every one of his stories. Just like at the theatre, there were always several »curtains«. Enquiries or even criticism was never in demand. That I had understood quite quickly.

Letting our relationship pass through my head now, I realize that I was a silly, totally uncritical listener, none but the uneducated decorator's apprentice in his father's shop in Linz, preparing for his »bread-and-butter job«, as »Adi« used to express it scornfully.

›What were »Adi's« objections to that? A secure job has always been a good thing, more so when thinking about children and family, too‹, and I do have my thoughts on that today.

»Family« was, of course, one of those subjects which would make »Adi« react rather crazy. His father, the customs official, beat him nearly every day and with utter brutality:

›Civil servant with a good education you shall become, like your father. A respected profession you shall learn – be diligent at school and orderly – otherwise you'll have another thrashing coming!‹ – A horror, this father, with civil servant ways, secure income and the airs and graces of a servant of state.

How very different was his mother, and »Adi« wore her locket on his heart by day and night. She idolized her son and the son loved his mother sincerely.

»Adi« cared for and looked after his mother for months, for weeks, daily until she died in his arms.

Often »Adi« had told me about Dr. Bloch who devotedly looked after his mother – a doctor for the poor and a Jew. There is in those days here and there anti-Semitism, but not to the extent of being after their lives. And »Adi« enthused about Dr. Bloch praising him to the skies, him the stunted Jew.

The word »school«, too, was such an emotive term. »Adi« didn't want anything to do with that institution – neither with pupils nor with teachers. The only exception was the professor of history Dr. Leopold Pötsch – »Adi« rather idolized him.

Now, in retrospect, while I am giving thought to our friendship, it comes to me, that »Adi« suppressed something.

Something terrible must have happened before his adolescence, meaning already during his childhood, which shadowed all his thinking and acting – the hated school, the slap-happy father with his tenure as a civil servant couldn't have been the only reason. Something must be there, conscious or subconscious, which influenced all of his actions.

One thing was totally clear and unmistakable – »Adi« was a completely self-centered person – and there was only one correct opinion, already with 16, 17, 18 years of age – solely his own one:

-     In talks he never backed down.

- There weren't any talks anyhow, only speeches, right out monologues.
- His opinion was actually cemented from the beginning, not to be modified in any way.
- A change of point of view was never possible, not even in the slightest tinge.

Never came to »Adi« the idea that his opinion could be wrong – even 99 from 100 people thinking differently would have had to submit to the one and only »insider«!

Democracy, majority decisions he put aside as an instrument of »prattlers« and »weaklings«.

Already in his youth here was only one principle valid for him, and that was the »principle of leadership«, seeing himself as the »Fuehrer of many peoples« and sometimes even as »Fuehrer of the whole World«. At first stated only as a dream – but soon expressed crystal-clear, real and unmistakable:

›**Uncompromising order by me, Adolf Hitler, by the one and only, and unconditional obedience by the others!**‹, was his slogan.

Only, there weren't any others, it was always only me August Kubizek – his only friend, »Gustl«, over the last four years. All the others he avoided, despised them, pushed them aside, didn't let anyone come near him.

The hard and fast principle of »Adi« was:
- Never admit to an error.
- Go all out only.
- Never question your own point of view!

The result:
No enhancement of thinking by new findings and understandings.

Thus:
Never learn from your own mistakes, never take a step backwards, much less a turnabout or change of path for tactical reasons in his reasoning – if necessary with temporary retreats and new advances – there was nothing like that!

That which distinguishes a high class boxer, a fight with ever new variations:
- go into the man

- retreat from the man
- turn left, turn right
- clinch, speed up
- recover, fight.

»Adi« didn't have command of any of this! – »Adi« only knew:

- into the ring and smack in the face!

He was never conscious of the fact, that with his way of acting, success and failure could be very close together – even high class boxers will lose, that's what the boxing history shows.

Now, for me Alfred Kubizek, there arises one question:

›Can anyone like »Adi« someday become a person of leadership, if he is already at the age of 16, 17, 18 so full of himself, that he will take advice from no one, is not prepared to include knowledge and experience of others into his own thoughts?

Can anyone like »Adi« become a great leader when he is even today, at the age of 19, already practicing for appearances before »millions«?‹

That happens before me, »Gustl«, daily who takes the place of the People thirsting for »Hitler's words«.

»Adi« practices nearly daily before this one-man audience, while demanding from his one listener, instead of the »imaginary crowds«, fidelity, loyalty, absence of criticism, and really unlimited enthusiasm! After his words, for his later aims, he needs neither friends nor »generals«!

In »Adi's« philosophy all people are to have only one task for existence:

›They exist only to obey
– a gifted »Fuehrer« like for instance me, Adolf Hitler!‹

I really do have to admit, however, that »Adi« has read everything that he could get hold of. His pride were over one hundred books which he read and understood exclusively thus, that he filtered and recapitulated only what served his dream of becoming a »Fuehrer« of what group ever. He was well informed about communists, socialists, loyalists to the emperor, advocate of a »Great German Reich« with all German speaking citizens, unions and Jews as well.

There was only one subject to which »Adi« was more reserved than was the case to other contents. In the past it seemed to me, that he, when it came to music, he would submit to the sounds of once heard strains than to play the nagging know-all.

To opera, Richard Wagner and theatre even I could give my opinion, because that was something I had knowledge of – entirely undoubtedly. In addition, I could play the piano quite well, was admitted to the music academy and was even allowed to give private piano lessons to daughters of the »high society«.

This had, however, an end with the opera »Rienzi«. In Roman history, having risen from the ordinary people, »Rienzi« was the secret star of »Adi«.

That the story of »Rienzi« ended rather sadly and dramatically, »Adi« didn't fancy at all. Because »Adi's« hero from the Roman people failed and was miserably burned!

… For how long I've been sitting here on the curb of the street, I don't know. How many people might have passed me by in the meantime? – I notice neither them, nor the elegant one- and two-horse carriages, drawn by marvellous horses – often occupied only by a coachman sitting on an elevated seat up front and two ladies behind – the coach, the most popular means of transport of the young 20th Century.

What will this Century bring?

›Will »Adi«, the »well-read with the iron will« play any part in the new future?‹ – a question torments my brain.

He really can talk, and what he says does make sense, and already today he is so convinced of himself that with his charisma and powers of persuasion, something might come of him – perhaps a politician?

Already now he masters in his speeches to me and to his imaginary audience the use of supporting gestures with his hands, fingers, arms and head – indeed, with his whole body – perfect measures, to take his perfectly phrased text to a total success. Everything had been prepared to the smallest detail days ahead, nothing was left to coincidence.

There were the eyes; they actually bound the »audience« into the present speech. The »audience« was really captivated by those eyes and the ever changing facial expression. Additional tension for the listener was created through longer pauses and a calculated lowering and raising of the voice.

The »Young Adolf Hitler« was a true master of speech already at the age of around 17, 18, 19 – just like a gifted violinist on his instrument.

The ceremony at the end of a speech was always the same:
- The audience, that is me, »Gustl«, rose from their seats and applauded enthusiastically.
- The speaker took a mouthful of water while wiping his black strand of hair from his drenched face.

A finish as every time, »audience« and speaker probably felt the same way – unmistakably – both sides appeared quite satisfied!

But »Adi« had to bury grandiloquent dreams, too:

Twice he didn't pass the exam for the Academy of Arts in Vienna. For him, completely shattering, him being so absolutely sure of his artistic talent – or did there become, in this case, a certain self conceitedness visible?

One thing now was for sure, too: »Adi« would probably never become a great artist!

Had he possibly realized after the »arts test disaster« that three irrefutable circumstances were contradictory to studying the arts?
- No high school qualification.
- No educational background in art.
- No outstanding talent.

Perhaps »Adi« could become an architect – or politician after all?

I myself was very often like in a trance when listening to my friend lecturing on politics. He always behaved as if there were 1000 listeners, and not only a single one – »Gustl Kubizek«!

Amazing how well »Adi« coped with his defeats at the Academy of Arts, only to devote himself even more to his books – unshakably convinced some day to become a great, mighty influential personality.

›My time will come!‹, he then used to say often.

As clearly and indisputably as »Adi« and I, too, his friend »Gustl« saw the person »Adolf Hitler« to become a famous contemporary in the near future, there were two things concerning hi that couldn't be any more contradictory:

1. Rural idyll and city
2. Girls as objects of desire and girls as enthralled nymphs of imagination.

»Thus I couldn't explain to myself on the one hand, *"a strange contradiction" in Adi's character for a long time.*

When the bright sun was shining into the lanes and a fresh, lively wind took the smell of the woods into the town, it drove him with an irresistible power out of the narrowness of the town and out into the meadows and Forests.

No sooner were we out, however, he assured me that it would be impossible for him to keep staying in the country. It would be terrible for him, once again having to live in a village such as Leonding was. Much as he loved nature, he was happy every time we returned to the familiar city.«[17]

Since I didn't dare ask the visionary Adolf Hitler about this contradiction, I looked for a simple, plausible explanation that would satisfy me:

»The village was, looking at it from this point of view, much too monotonous and too unimportant, too insignificant and therefore for his boundless need to occupy himself with everything, much too unproductive.«[18]

Here on my curbstone by a lively street, I am beginning to »see the light«:

If I accept the last sentence, it does not supply a solution to the afore emphasized contradiction of »rural idyll« versus »city«.

Now, as it is getting dark, and the sentinels are lighting the gas lanterns, an insight is lighting up in me as well:

- when »Adi« flees from the city to the rural idyll
- and, as soon as the rural idyll surrounds him, again rushes in the direction of the city, then this is indeed a contradiction!

It is becoming clear for me: **»Adi« is afraid!**

---

[17] *August Kubizek, Adolf Hitler – Mein Jugendfreund. Publishing house Leopold Stocker, Graz [1953], p. 32*

[18] *ibidem*

The otherwise so self confident 19-years old is afraid of the rural idyll – he actually dreads his home village of Leonding.

When actually the seldom conversation came to the rural Leonding, »Adi« always appeared to me taciturn and off-putting, which even more confirms my before made statement.

Also the **second unsolved contradiction** in the character of my friend becomes more and more clear to me, because he encounters adolescent girls in a very different manner.

Even though »Adi« is a handsome, slender youth, and daily on our walks the girls are making eyes at him, he did never seek closer contact with any one of them.

The young ladies never wink at me, only at »Adi«, I must admit frankly. I must say that I am a bit disappointed, but in no way envious of »Adi's« success with the ladies.

How often could »Adi« have got more out of such unmistakable demonstrations of sympathy, and without any effort at that.

›How unjust are the ways of life‹, I am thinking sitting on my curb.

If only that »strapping« lady in her pink dress and dainty umbrella had pointed at me, while mounting the coach at the side of her mother. If only that open, hearty smile could have been for me – but no, it was directed at »Adi« – and he looked away, just walked on, even though these advances were absolutely clear and not to be overlooked by anyone – least of all by »Adi« himself!

›Come now, »Gustl«, let's go‹, was the only comment.

›How unjust this world is!‹

Thus »Adi« has got a fictitious love, a love that goes on only in his imaginations. Her name is Stefanie and she often walks with her mother: a pretty 18-year old with luxuriant blonde hair and an immaculate body – admittedly.

›Stefanie is my great love, though I wouldn't even kiss or touch her. Our love is sacred and so pure – and therefore so difficult to describe with worldly words‹, so says this raving youth in love.

Quite strange, refuses the strapping young beauties with their zest for life his bed, prefers to revel for days in monologues, raising up to the »level of heavens« and conjuring the purity of his love and to condemn carnal lust as being unclean.

Incredible, »Adi« prefers a girl from Linz to whom he had never spoken and probably never will, a girl that hasn't the faintest idea of his adoration – this only in thought to experience and thus completely unrequited love – prefers her to worldly beauties who seriously want to caress him.

›Very unusual for a 19-year old, healthy normal man‹, I thus contemplate,

›or is »Adi« in his relationship to the other sex possibly neither **healthy** nor **normal**?‹

Thoughts that I would never dare to have if »Adi« were anywhere near me: Is this contradiction, to put sexual practices to the test by actions or merely enthusiastic indulgence on »cloud number nine«, connected to that terrible childhood experience which suddenly opens up for my insight and explanation of the strange behaviour of my friend an entirely new track?

So I was extremely astonished that, when it must have irresistibly »burned in his trousers«, one day he dragged me straight into the red light district, where the girls lazed in the »shop windows«, presenting their naked legs and breasts. »Adi« took my arm and said to my huge amazement:

» ›Come on, Gustl, just this once we do have to survey the 'den of iniquity'.‹ «[19]*

So we proceeded along the poorly lit Spittelbergstrasse down to Burgstrasse. We never stopped anywhere nor did we talk to any of the girls.

Everyone again only registered »Adi«, not me – smiled at him temptingly. Thus we passed the windows twice, because we turned around and repeated our walk, until we then turned into Westbahnstrasse.

›Good for nothing whores all of them‹, »Adi« summarized the rare experience and added,

›in these poor creatures the »flame of life« has long gone out!‹

Today, in retrospect, this summary and assessment of our unique experience appears highly questionable to me.

---

[19] *August Kubizek – Mein Jugendfreund. Publishing house Leopold Stocker, Graz [1953], p. 235*

Every other youth would have, after viewing the half naked, and partly very pretty girls, reacted entirely different – that is becoming clear to me today!

Is possibly that terrible experience from childhood days in the village of Leonding present once again, which like a conditioned reflex immediately turns the word »sex« from »normal« to »abnormal«, giving no chance to an unprejudiced way of looking at things, as would be usual with youths? Is there today something that makes »Adi« afraid of himself and afraid of me, his best friend? I, »Gustl« am now quite sure of that!

While I am now coming to the end of my contemplation, in the bustling street of Vienna in 1908, one thing has become clear to me: Now that I've had the opportunity to again think everything over, the face of my friend has nearly vanished, only still to be perceived as a shadowy picture.

Summarizing I must discover for myself, that despite our four years together, I do not really know my friend. This becomes especially clear when thinking of two school class photos which »Adi« showed me:

On one of them, in 1899, in the fourth grade of primary school in Leonding, »Adi« is standing in the top row and there in the middle. On the other photo, in 1901, in first form of grammar school in Linz, »Adi« is still in the top row – but here on the extreme right.

*»Adi's face on these photos is always the same. Even though a considerable stretch of time lies between these two photos, it is still the same, strange face, as if it hadn't changed any. I think, that therein already, yet completely instinctive, that strange consequence shows, that **not-being-able-to-change**, which appears to as a substantial trait of character of the young Hitler.«*[20]

›Estranged he has become to me, my friend »Adi« – or has my friend actually always been a stranger to me, and I, the decorator's apprentice, haven't even noticed for all that »applause blarney«?‹

All this has now become clear to me, while in thought on that street curbstone in the bustle of the Vienna of 1908.

---

[20] *cf August Kubizek, Adolf Hitler – Mein Jugendfreund. Publishing house Leopold Stocker, Graz [1953], p. 27*

Even though still my best friend, in my memory »Adi« will appear from now on as:

- the »stranger« from Leonding
- the »stranger« from Linz and also
- the »stranger« from Vienna!

There is only one last question left for me, Alfred Kubizek:

›What else has God planned? What has God in mind with this Adolf Hitler?‹

»*What does God want with this man?*«[21]

Visiting the Jewish Prostitute Rebecca – »Adi's« first amorous adventure comes to a fiasco and triggers his hate of Jews and enmity towards women

"Today it has to be!"

I have decided. I have finally made up my mind to do what every young man does – it was like that in the olden days, it will be like that tomorrow and it is just so today. I, »Adi«, complete name Adolf Hitler, have decided to do it today.

Today I will go to a lady of whom all the 17-, 18- and 19-years old who went there are delighted. They all talk about the dark-haired Rebecca who treats the young gentlemen so thoughtfully, as if she had to perform the duties as a mother. But you can hardly call the task about which it is today, the duties as a mother – it is rather that on this day I want to become a »real man«, to experience for the first time what it actually is like with a woman – stark naked both of us – as God created us – and between my legs it is really beginning to tingle.

"My God, just to think of those big boobs and strapping buttocks of Rebecca, one feels all warm inside", and my already a bit too tight pants are suspiciously bulging at the front.

---

[21] cf *August Kubizek, Adolf Hitler – Mein Jugendfreund. Publishing house Leopold Stocker, Graz [1953], p. 37*

My friend Kubizek has already told how the event takes place – he has already been to Rebecca three times.

"Long black hair and a snow-white skin she has – all sensual dark eyes and the full lips of a lovely mouth made for kissing, with which she actually does kiss properly. She kisses on the cheeks, on the mouth and…", it was enough to make me sick when I come to think of how »Gustl« explained, how she all voluptuously nearly swallowed his »zippedeus«.

"My God", said Kubizek,

"that really hammered in your sac!"

»Gustl« has kept his ears open: No one who had been with her ever became ill. That, of course, was reassuring – unthinkable if you had to see a doctor because of a burning in your »zippedeus«. One does hear such a lot of what happens in the moral quagmire of the big city, I do have to be absolutely sure!

Rebecca is specialized on introducing young hotheads into the art of love. She knows that these youngsters are coming for the first time, and this »fresh meat« isn't yet spoiled and intertwined with disease. Rebecca serves the 17- to 25-year olds only, and there is the rumour, that it is a pleasure for her to offer her services – that she actually enjoys sex with the boys.

She isn't all that big, so that her giant breasts clearly protrude. They fit to the somewhat full bottom, because these curves are conspicuously noticeable because of her far renown wasp waist.

»Gustl« was especially enthusiastic about her wearing nearly transparent oriental clothes, which permitted to first take a glance into the low neckline with the giant breasts, to then let the eyes wander lower to the lovely slender legs that ended in small, high-heeled slippers.

First of all »Gustl« had to get into a kidney shaped bath tub – to be washed down from head to toe. She really is clean, that Rebecca, and that she demands of her guests, too.

Was the »zippedeus« already highly sensitized in the warm water of the tub as soon as Rebecca's hands touched the body with the sponge – so every »zippedeus« faded from the scene as soon as she washed off the remains of soap with ice-cold water. But in the supersized bed, the unpleasant water hose was quickly forgotten she brought the »good one« back to life once more.

"If you believe it or not, »Adi« she actually praised my »zippe«, saying, and I quote:

›That's a cute one, and not too big, but a real cuddly one to play with.‹

And all the time I had been worrying if my »centimetre-monster« wouldn't be discarded as useless, but no, she cuddled up to my body and gently fondled me all over, so that I felt to be on »cloud number nine«. She made me feel as my »little one« was the »greatest«", and after taking a short breath »Gustl« continued with his exciting story.

"In everything she did, she was really loving, nearly motherly. When she tried a Vienna accent with her dark, soft voice – you wouldn't recognize her as »lady of easy virtue«, the known-all-over-town prostitute!"

"That is really great", I, »Adi«, am thinking happily.

If she was able to enlarge »Gustl's« midget by encouragement, she will show understanding for me, too. Even if my »zippedeus« compared to »Gustl's« is not to be called a midget, mine really has taken on quite a strange shape – since the day when I, the nine-year old, was bitten in the penis by that billy goat!

Wait and see. If the motherly Rebecca has an understanding for my unusual-looking reproduction gadget, the later, my above all dearly loved Stefanie may accept my sex toy, yes, perhaps even love it.

Even »Gustl« I have never shown that strange thing – much too great was my fear and feeling of shame at the reaction to be expected!

While his »thingy« daily danced before my eyes, because he loved to run around the house naked, and I looked up to him I irritation, he stated grinning:

"That's the way God has created us, isn't it", and he wasn't at all insulted, when I seriously showed outrage and talked about it »not being seemly«.

"So this today is the first »real test« of the young Hitler in »sex matters«", I try to convince myself.

Only the terrible thing is, that you can in no way prepare yourself for the coming, can take no influence on it – when I do value so much to adapt to every situation so that I am in command at any time.

… So I am standing in front of Door No. 3 of House No. 19 of the red light district of Vienna.

"In addition to this, there is the further unknown that I don't even know Rebecca, have never seen her", I diagnose for myself, assessing my situation.

Here on the first floor, the girls are in their rooms, and don't flirt around like it can be seen on the ground floor.

And there I stand with my card on which it says:
17th of November 1908, 7 p.m., Rebecca.

The little card with the appointment I had to get a few days in advance under a cover address at an old lady's. When I left she winked at me with her steel-blue eyes, which really didn't fit to the ocean of wrinkles on her ancient face.

"Right on, young man, no fears – Rebecca doesn't bite!", and there was a slight giggle to be heard from the old lady, somehow encouraging, and by no means unpleasant.

So the I gather all my courage – the little card in my left hand – a soft knock on door No. 3, as from the church steeple nearby the clock strikes a dull seven exactly.

Still the somewhat »smoky«, pleasant sounding voice can be clearly heard:

"Do come in", and I, »Adi«, walk determined into the room and pull the door into the lock shut behind me.

"Well, my boy, how are you?" the »smoky«, pleasant voice says, and turning around to me, Rebecca beams at me with her dark eyes.

"What is your name, what do they call you?"

"Good evening, Madam, my name is »Adi«, and thank you so much for sparing some time for me."

"Well, my handsome young lad that is actually my task, to spare time. Just call me Rebecca, everyone does."

"Gladly, Madam – um – Rebecca", and my heart is still beating as if there were steam hammers in my chest.

"Who was it that brought you to me, »Adi«?"

"It was »Gustl«, my friend, he told me of you."

"Ah, »Gustl«, nice boy, knows a lot about music! – but now, off with those duds, »Adi«, – not so bashful! Here for the first time, I guess, – no need to be afraid, just do as if I were your big sister. You'll see that it can be quite nice with a »new sister«. – So off with your clothes and into the small tub next door. There's also a candle burning for the romantic hour. Perhaps you'll feel better if not everything is seen at once. A bit of twilight glow makes it a lot easier to get to know one another!"

In the reception room, too, that seems to consist only of a supersized bed – with two chairs, a small table and two bedside cabinets – in the evening there too is a dimmed lamp spreading pink light. Heavy silk curtains part the small homely room from the ensuing night outside.

With my still fluttering heart I go to the room next door. There are actually only two small kidney shaped tubs there. One is filled with warm water and a lot of suds. The other one is empty with the hose for the ice-cold water dangling in the air! It really makes ones hair stand on end when thinking of »Gustl's« warning words.

"Now quickly off with the clothes – into the tub and dive with the body under the lather – the lower part of the body at least", I say to myself to take a bit of courage and am ashamed of my nakedness.

And already she comes floating along!

"My God!", I exclaim. She is wearing nothing but small triangular panties, and the mighty breasts bob up and down with every step – protruding far ahead, promoted by the high-heel house slippers.

"Well, »Adi«, do you like me?" – and bending over she immediately begins to wash my shoulders with the sponge, standing in front of me and beaming at me.

"Well, »Adi«, what do you say?"

"Simply phenomenal, Madam – um – Miss Rebecca. I can't express in words how beautiful you are, much more beautiful than »Gustl« described to me."

Fascinated I watch Rebecca's »giant melons« swinging totally uncontrolled to and fro in front of my face. For a moment I am actually enthralled by this beautiful woman feeling more pleasure than fear – of what is still to come.

"Say, Miss Rebecca, may I ask you a question?"

"Whatever you wish and I will answer you, my boy."

"Are all Jewish ladies as pretty as you are, Miss Rebecca? For you had told my friend »Kubi«, that you are of Jewish nationality."

"No, no, no, my dear »Adi«, I am of Austrian nationality, with a real passport – it's only my faith that is Jewish – and pretty are all Jewish women!", and her dark voice sounds pleasantly warn, confidence extremely inspiring.

She interrupts the washing procedure, beams at me again, tenderly kisses my forehead, and starts at the chest – and I blurt out:

"That does tickle!", as she caresses my nipples with small, circular movements.

"Now, »Adi«, stand up straight, we shall now admire your »zippedeus«. Judging by your big nose, it must be a »really mighty thing«." – And the curiosity of the young woman is unmistakable.

" ›By the length of a man's beak is shown, how long his »willy« sure has grown‹, that's an ancient saying", and she bursts out laughing, and »Adi«, too, laughs, but only really briefly. And that is quite unusual for him, because normally he doesn't laugh at all –

and for the rest of his future life
he will never again laugh heartily!

"For the love of God, what is that supposed to be?" – Rebecca suddenly exclaims, and it sounds shocked.

Standing up, »Adi's« penis becomes visible, still more or less covered in suds, still at once recognizable for the experienced labouress of love:

"There is something wrong with that »thing«!"

"Mr. »Adi«", and she employs the non familiar »Sie«[22],

"into the other tub at once!", the call comes in the harsh imperious tone. Immediately she begins to squirt with the water hose, exclusively aiming at belly and »zippedeus«.

In a second all my »male feelings« have disappeared – now the »thing« just hangs around there, miserably. Actually it is two »things« – a really strange shape for a penis, I am aware of that!

---

[22] *»Sie«: German formal way of address between strangers, equivalent to the formal »one« in English.*

I am paralyzed with fright, standing stiff as a board in the bath tub, staring at the »motherly beloved for one night« terrified with eyes wide open.

Indeed, what is there presented to the »youth spoilt nymph« is actually a »horror appliance« and not the penis of a nineteen-year old summoning for games.

The top half seems quite normal – but then it can clearly be seen, how the bite of the billy goat mutilated my, that of a nine-year old, genital:

- The bite didn't cover entirely the whole width of the penis (Illus. 5, page 80), so that the lower half of the penis transformed – actually split up lengthwise, into a »bright scarlet left bulb«, and to the right into a »black, dangling lobe of skin, void of blood« (Illus. 6, page 80).

A really gruesome sight that is for every woman longing for love – especially for an untouched virgin at first contact!

The knife-sharp lower incisors (Illus. 7, on the left, page 80), sliced my little penis, if you want to say so, into three parts!

The lower teeth struck firmly against the cartilage of the upper bone plate in the mouth of the billy goat, without completely severing the penis.

Since then, the urine meanders from the damaged urethra, somewhat central, under the left piece of cartilage and to the right over the black lobe of skin, in which the supply of blood was nearly completely interrupted.

Our then general practitioner, Dr. Bloch, immediately examined the fresh wound, but strongly advised against any kind of operation which would only bring about further suffering, but no improvement.

Even though that short-in-growth Jew couldn't help me any, I am to this day thankful for his discretion – not a breath of a word passed his lips as to the subject of mutilation of the penis of the nine-year old Adolf Hitler, called »Adi« from Leonding.While these thoughts race through my head within fractions of seconds, the »love mistress Rebecca« has planted herself in front of me, hands propped on her hips – with a piercing glare looking into my eyes.I myself am still standing stiff as a board in the tub, incapable of any movement.

..... "I, too, Immo, on my two million light years distant lookout in the Andromeda Galaxy, must have taken on the piercing look of the »love mistress Rebecca«, too, because my father is watching me in surprise, even appearing a bit disturbed.

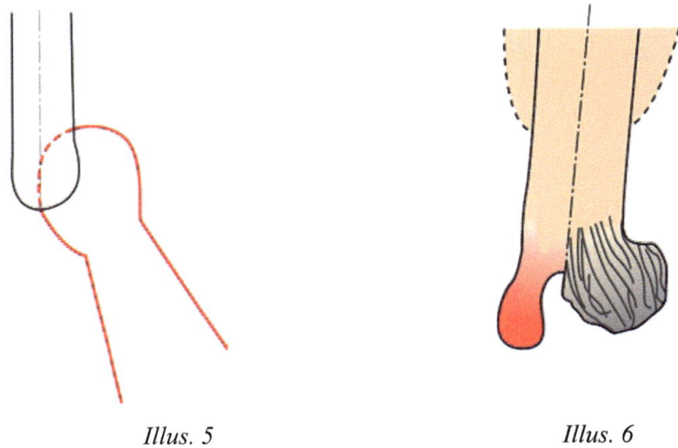

Illus. 5   *Illus. 6*

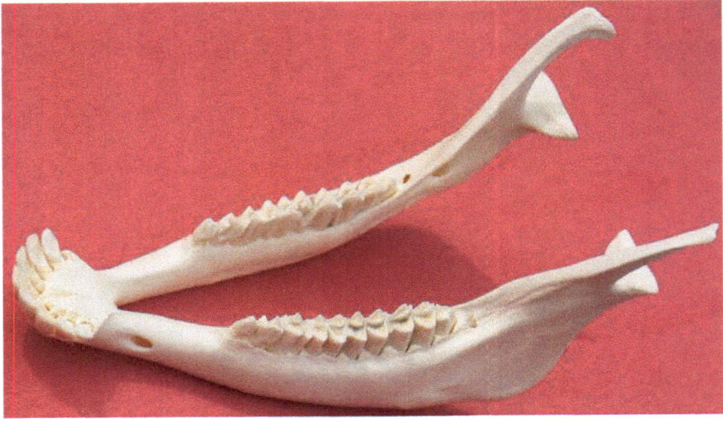

Illus. 7

Still we notice the change in the otherwise so self confident youthful Adolf Hitler:

A 19-year old boy in his first love adventure

- white as a sheet in his face
- his glance lowered to the floor
- arms hanging loosely at his sides
- shoulders bent to the front:

A youth trembling with fear and shame, a loser and not a winner – and by no means the self confident young Mister Hitler, the one he always wanted to be when hastening after his beloved Stefanie, waving around his ivory-clad little walking stick.

This is the essential of the observations made by both of us, by father and son, on the far distant planet of »Tora« after the assessment of the scene in the flat of the Jewish lady Rebecca!"
.....

Suddenly »black Rebecca« turns around

- races into the other room
- returns in a second, covered in a dressing gown
- »plants« herself in front of the still stiff as a board »Adi«
- points he outstretched arm and index finger at the »miserable thing«, that a gone wild billy goat had mutilated ten years ago on that meadow in Leonding!

With flashing eyes the »whore Rebecca« now starts screaming, void of any motherly charisma:

"You Spawn of Satan! How dare you appear here with that horrible »gadget«!

Do you want my ruin? What do you think will happen if the word gets around:

- Rebecca with her good reputation serves a leper!
- Do you want to infect all of us?
- Have you ever heard of the term »mercy killing«?
- Such »diseased« people like you should be separated, locked up – before they infest the whole of the people!
- Everything that is ill, not worthy of life, not viable, has to go.

I never want to hear your name again, and don't you dare come here anymore!

- The day will come when cripples like you will be hunted down and isolated!

Just wait, you'll get to know it! Hit the road, scram and get out of my life! Grab your clothes! – there, that's where the door is!"

»Adi« begins to move. As fast as never before he jumps into his underpants, shirt, trousers and shoes. Jacket and undershirt under his arm he storms out into the street.

"Here, you idiot, your dirty socks", and Rebecca throws them after him down the stairs.

»Adi« knows only one goal: Out of this house, away from the wretched red-light district, out into nature – into the nearby city park. The young Mister Hitler races off – as if pursued by »furies«.

It is November, the leaves are falling and he immediately feels the fresh wind that is blowing today. All of a sudden it begins to rain, stronger and stronger, a real cloudburst!

»Adi« jerks his hands towards the sky.

"Rain, my dear rain", he shouts,

"wash me clean of this sink of iniquity!"

Again he raises his arms to the sky – and the rain beats down – and the weather is noisy!

But then everything is drowned by the cry of the young man with his arms raised to the sky – drenched to the bone, the water streaming over his black hair:

"You wicket woman, you whose name I will never again mention.

- You have insulted me, me Adolf Hitler, who will once rule over whole peoples.

- You, woman, are so unfathomably bad, as only the devil can figure. Yes, the devil's handiwork is what you are!

- And the rabble that has created you will be met by my anathema some day!

- I am a leper, you say, and euthanasia shall devour me, in the sense of exterminating all unworthy life.

- You, woman, have with your own depravity provoked your own doom!

- That which you have intended for me, will now devour you and your kind!

As one Jewish woman is thus bad, the whole »riff-raff« of Jews must be bad, too! So those are in the right who wish the Jews to be struck by the plague!

Even worse:

- You, bad Jew woman and your rabble, you shall suffer until judgment day!
- I, Adolf Hitler, do not believe in God, but I swear to employ all of my power to one day fulfill this oath!"

And the young man once more throws his arms up to the sky and from his innermost his cry comes – against the wind and the strong rain:

"Death to you, Jewish whore and to your entire people! – Providence will lead me and fit all the rest into place!"

… His thoughts went haywire.

"Friend »Gustl« will be arriving shortly", it suddenly came over him!

"Away as quickly as possible. Too great is the danger that anything of the »red light debacle« becomes public. Off and away from the Stumpergasse! And it is high time, too, to go own ways, without the student of music Alfred Kubizek!"

Young Hitler rushes home, packs his things and next morning hastily bids farewell with the following words:

"Good bye, Mrs. Zakreys, here is my part of the rent."

"But Mr. Kubizek will be arriving! Whatever shall I tell him? What is your new address, Mister Hitler?"

"I'll arrange that with Mr. Kubizek myself, all the best to you, Mrs. Zakreys."

And as if in a soliloquy he murmurs not audible but to himself:

"Life goes on without you, »Gustl«. I'll manage on my own. I don't need a friend!"

The juvenile Hitler is in need of being alone – to start anew in the bustle of the crowd of 2,000,000. He wants to be beyond reach of all who know him – for family acquaintances and for his friend, too! The whore Rebecca forces him to go underground – to make himself invisible – untraceable for everyone.

And a young man, called »Adi« with family name Adolf Hitler leaves Stumpergasse 29 in the district of Mariahilf in the metropolis of Vienna on the 18th of November of the year 1908 and disappears groaning under the weight of his book laden suitcases.

Hitler and his Niece »Geli« –
The love-crazed Hitler and the clever girl from Linz

"Well, »Geli«, how do you like it here with me in your new home?", the »Fuehrer« of the National Socialist Party of Germany begins the conversation.

"It's good, Uncle »Alf«, I like it very much – and thank you so much for taking me into your nine room house on Prinzregenten Square 16 here in Munich. I do thank you very much, especially for the nice corner room with the view on Prinzregenten Theatre. It is quite handy if we want to see each other.

Before this, you, Uncle, in Thierschstrasse No. 41, I in the English Garden – it was actually a bit complicated. Now everything is much easier and a lot more beautiful – I really do feel comfortable here with you!"

And uncle »Alf« and his ward »Geli« are sitting on a big sofa, drinking tea and looking into the blazing flames of the open fireplace. Outside there is snow already and inside it is homely warm in January of the year 1932.

»Geli«, with her correct name of Angela Maria Raubal, is the daughter of Angela Raubal, a half-sister of Adolf Hitler. Already since 1923 uncle »Alf«, as he is affectionately called by his charge, is her official guardian.

Now both of them are sitting on the huge sofa, wearing pyjamas, with »Geli« having her knees drawn up and her arms around them.

The uncle is leant back, so that he is now more lying down than sitting, comfortably on two cushions which »Geli« has propped him up with. There is soft music from the gramophone which, together with the crackling of the burning birch wood accompanies the homely atmosphere.

"Another pot of tea, Herr Hitler?" asks Mrs. Winter, the wife of the janitor, who suddenly enters the room.

"Is there enough wood for the fire place? Or shall my husband fetch some more? Perhaps some beech wood, it burns longer", and she is about to pour some tea. But »Geli« says:

"Thank you, Mrs. Winter, but I'll serve the uncle myself – and thank you so much for the lovely homemade biscuits."

"And I, too, say thanks so much, Mrs. Winter, for the fire wood and the tea, everything there in sufficient amount. The warmer under the tea pot will keep it warm for hours. There is enough fire wood, too, so that we could actually overwinter.", Hitler tries a little joke.

"And do close the door behind you, we won't be needing you any more today, it's 7 p.m. after all – good night", with that the female part of the janitor couple is dismissed.

One realizes that Hitler wants to be undisturbed with his niece.

"Good night Herr Hitler, good night Miss »Geli«", and the impressive double door is slammed shut audibly.

The uncle and his niece are alone.

"Say, »Geli« how do you imagine your further future to be? You are already a real woman at 22 years of age – and a beautiful one at that!"

"Come now, Uncle, are you flirting with me? I think that I'll make a passable singer and can then fend for myself."

Both are silent for a while, but the uncle comes back to the subject.

"Can't you perhaps imagine staying with me altogether – I mean forever – »Little Geli«?"

"Oh dear, Uncle, how do you think that is going to work out? Am I to become »Mrs. Chancellor of the Reich«? That you, Uncle, are going to be the chancellor of the German Reich one day, after your

NSDAP[23] last autumn has already become second strongest party in the country, is as certain as the sunrise.

I could very exactly observe your path to power. Especially impressive was that you took me on your campaign journeys every time – and I, »Little Geli«, have met such a lot of important and rich men and their wives, too.

The Nuremberg Rally in 1927, too, to which you had invited me, was great experience, even though the trip to the big and well known cities of Bayreuth, Weimar, Berlin and Hamburg were the actual peak. You know, Uncle, that I don't care much for politics, but the way your driver, Mr. Rudolf Heß, explained everything, indeed was a special experience for the uneducated Miss Angela Raubal.

With mother, who had then come along, it was different. For her it wasn't the tour of the cities which was the highest, no, for her the climax was the up and coming party, the NSDAP with its »Fuehrer«, my famous uncle", and »Geli« cuddles up to her uncle, as in gratitude, real closely!

"You see, »Geli« you have charmed all my party members – Heß, Goebbels, Göring – you've enchanted them all, you have won them as friends for yourself, everyone likes you – even the women.

Both of them paused for a moment to pursue their own thoughts – but then the uncle comes to the actual nucleus of today's talk. He takes a deep breath as if to boost his courage and then takes up the dialog once again.

"Can't you imagine staying with me forever, with your uncle »Alfi«? You don't have to be newly introduced into our »society«, everyone knows you, and because you are so open, honest and altogether natural, everyone will accept you.

You are now 22, and we have known each other for such a long time. Now is, of course, the right time to consider, yes, to decide if you are going to stay with me forever and if there can be more between us than the so far uncle-niece-relationship!"

And »Geli« answers absolutely spontaneous:

---

[23] *NSDAP – National Socialist Labour Party, 1920-1945. Head of Party since 1921 was the later Chancellor of the Reich, Adolf Hitler.*

"But Uncle, then I would have to come into your bed!"

"That is just »Geli« the way she is! She doesn't beat about the bush!", the uncle thinks to himself, sensing a feeling that it wasn't altogether a clear rejection.

"But, Uncle, you do know," »Geli« takes the word again,

"you know, that I'm still a virgin", and she blushes, visibly, all over her face.

"Now, that shouldn't really be a problem", Uncle »Alfi« answers quick-witted,

"that is something we can quickly change … ha, ha," and he slaps his thighs, as if to again reward himself for the new joke.

Both pause, just as if having to reassess the situation each one for themselves.

"You know, Uncle," »Geli« starts anew,

"you know that I didn't even have anything with my fiancé, Ferdinand Goldstein, to the day when you gave him, the founder of the SS with the party number 49, the boot. Such was your anger when he asked for my hand in marriage.

Yes, Uncle, that is how I am – a big mouth to all topics, but my »femininity« will reach only the one who has married me – a bit old fashioned, isn't it, uncle »Alfi«?"

"No, no, »Geli«, I am quite of the same opinion. The »thing« between man and woman is really something »holy«, and the way you do it is quite alright: Wait for the night after the wedding – like in ancient times – old-fashioned perhaps, but nowadays modern again, too!"

"Well", »Geli« continues the conversation, as if she doesn't want to stand for appearing like a little »sexual silly billy«.

"Well, Uncle, I do know just a little bit about sex from Mum, and there also, when I was nine years old, was my school friend Karlchen.

Karlchen always picked me up at Mum's place to go and play »cuckoo«. Karlchen then always pulled off his trousers and my panties had to go, too. Then he lay down in the hay on top of me and kept fidgeting around in a funny way – just like an »old billy goat«, ha, ha, ha", and she roars with laughter.

"›That's the way Mum and Dad do it‹, Karlchen used to explain and then asked of me to groan, because that's what his mum did, too. According to Karlchen's words, she used to groan something terrible, and Karlchen never was quite sure whether it was from pain or from pure pleasure!

Und Karlchen kept on fidgeting around on me, like a genuine billy goat!"

While the uncle still had himself under control during the whole of the children's story, it now really burst out of him:

"For God's sake, »Geli«, don't mention billy goats to me!", the uncle hissed in barely suppressed fury.

»Geli« is really taken aback, as the word was to be merely a funny comparison. But the strong-willed young woman immediately gets a grip on herself and continues quite freely:

"Karlchen's »willy« just jangled around in the air, and I didn't at all feel like touching that tiny thing – which really wasn't necessary, because Karlchen never asked me to.

Two years late it was a different matter. I was eleven and there was Franz'l – three grades higher. Franz'l liked me and always hugged me, just like grown-ups do when meeting, pressing his cheek quite friendly against mine.

›That's what you do when you like one another‹, he used to give as an explanation.

Then we often went for walks in the woods, and one day it happened: Franz'l took another careful look around to see if the coast were clear and if no other persons were near.

›Come on, »Geli« see what a toy I've got for you‹, drags me behind a bush, opens his fly and pulls out his »willy«.

Actually I should have cried out in dismay and shame, but no, to my own surprise all I uttered was:

›Wow, what a »thingy«!‹

Despite Franz'l being only a little bit bigger than I, his »zippedeus« appeared to me to be enormous, because whenever we girls used to talk about the proportions of our boys' »most precious possession«, the rule was actually:
-    Little boys have »little ones«!
-    Big boys have »big ones«!

›Come on, »Geli«, play around a bit‹, and he put my small hand on it, and in that way I learnt to cause him pleasure, with Franz'l groaning loudly each time. He groaned so terribly, that I couldn't help but ask myself if those were the sounds one makes when dying.

›You don't become pregnant from that‹, Franz'l then used to laugh.

We had this game nearly every day, and so long, until some fluid shot out the front. Only then did he stop groaning.

Following that, we used to walk a bit, with arms wrapped tightly around one another, like a real courting couple. Only when people out for a walk appeared, did we stroll separated, all well-mannered, as if both of us were simply »innocent little angels«!"

"That is some story, »Geli«", and the uncle takes the girl's hand and puts it on his thigh, just like the children probably did.

"That is something with which the two of us could start, to find out if the »cuckoo game« pleases us, too." And suddenly the uncle grabs »Geli's« well developed breasts and begins to voluptuously make grunting groans.

"You see, Uncle, that's what Franz'l always did, too − grabbed my breasts, they even then were already quite developed − and then he groaned just as you are doing now, Uncle »Alfi«!"

Just as »Geli« wants to grab the uncle in the crotch, because the pyjama trousers are already bulging mightily which therefore is for the young and, as well aroused, girl attractive, nearly inviting. But in this moment the uncle abruptly halts the searching, on discovery going curious little hand! He seizes her wrist in a firm grip, his thoughts going into a rush:

In his political speeches he always had prepared everything − to the last dot over the »i«. He knows in all probability how the campaign event is going to proceed. Every detail rehearsed in mind and in practice, too. The »great master« of rhetoric, Adolf Hitler, can exactly judge his audience. That is why his success at elections is so phenomenal. He was never mistaken. His predictions always hit home to one hundred percent.

But today, in togetherness with his niece, the future mighty »Fuehrer« of the Germans is completely dominated by his fears:

He is in no way capable of assessing what is going to happen within the next minutes, yes, even seconds.

"Now the moment has come in which my fate and that of »Geli«, too, is going to be decided!

That damned billy goat!"

The uncle murmurs − Germany's most famous uncle.

»Geli« only detects the word »billy goat« from the stuttering murmurs of her uncle and asks amused and smiling:

"But Uncle, whatever is the matter with that billy goat? Is it by chance a billy goat standing between the future »Fuehrer« of the Germans and his niece, or is it a kind of coat of arms in your political party?"

"No, no, »Geli«, no coat of arms, but you will see that this billy goat has something to do with both of us. If he will actually come between us, the next minutes will show!"

"Oh, Uncle, don't keep us in suspense, I'm not a child anymore and can take quite a bit. Resolve the secret. I'm all ears. Don't keep me on tenterhooks, or we'll never come to our »main feature«!"

The uncle has now positioned himself bolt upright, his chest pushed forward, supported by an extremely bent hollow back. He straightens out the trousers of his pyjamas − the pert tent in his crotch isn't there anymore, has completely disappeared.

The sensuality laden, and by »Geli« provoked eroticized mood, caused by two little children's stories, has gone altogether, too. It is unmistakable, that he whole of the evening togetherness of the two in conversation, has entered a decisive phase.

The almighty Adolf Hitler is gasping for breath – totally meek, the otherwise so »mighty voice«, drinks hastily three gulps of tea, clears his throat and begins:

"»Geli«, my beloved child, my darling, my »one and only«, I really don't know how to tell you, I'm somehow helpless and so I'll make it really short: There is a problem, a really big one, of which you, little »Geli«, can't have any idea", and the all over the country well known politician, before whom the masses tremble, is speechless − speechless to a little girl he loves!

"But uncle, you are otherwise always so brave, fear nobody, don't even run away when your friends are beaten bloody by the brutal communists!"

90

"My dearest »Geli«, here it is not about »beating«, but about »biting«!"

"But uncle »Alfi«, you are not trying to tell you that you were bitten by a billy goat – dogs that can really bite rather mean, I've heard of, but I've never come across a vicious billy goat!"

The normally so word powerful Adolf Hitler for the time being doesn't know what to say – gathers all his courage and begins anew:

"And yet, beloved niece, there is such a thing, even though it may sound like a fairytale from the lands of the Indians written by the glorious Karl May. So listen:

When I was a little boy in my home town Leonding, just on nine years old, we wanted to go into the holidays with a really dramatic start, something really big – my school friends and I. A test of courage it was to be:

»Who is going to piddle the billy goat on the meadow of Leonding into its mouth?«

No one dared, except I, »Adi«! And then it happened:

That huge snout of the »monster« bit me in the »zippedeus«!

Yes, that was then, some 33 years ago, the cause of what you see here as a result:

My penis looks all weird, and not anywhere like the one you know from your friend Franz'l!"

The uncle is as white as a wall in the face, and the question that would decide everything and demands an answer is:
- Will the revenge of the billy goat follow me all my life?
- Will I, the great Adolf Hitler and soon to be the most powerful man of our beloved German Fatherland, cringe with fear like a puppy?
- Will the nasty billy goat retaliate mercilessly – each time that I as much as come close to a beautiful woman?"

"But Uncle", »Geli's« voice is heard sounding somewhat like that of her mother when wanting to console a child after a bad dream.

"But Uncle, it can't be that bad really; let's have a look at the »thingy«. You can always better talk about something that you know the about something you don't know. Fear not, Uncle »Alfi«

I've already seen »zippedeuses«, as you know. So you won't be able to frighten me either!

Come on, Uncle, »no fear, out with the dear« – ha, ha, it even rhymes!", »Geli« tries to lighten up the depressed mood by that little joke.

"So, »Geli«, gather all your strength, I'll do it!"

The uncle stands up, pulls up the jacket of the pyjamas and garbs it with his teeth.

"Well, the belly already looks quite good, Uncle »Alf« – beyond any reproach!"

»Geli« can't go on, because the trousers have already been dropped – lie on the ground – and there it dangles, »**the one mutilated by a billy goat**«!

The »new strong man« of the German people closes his eyes and sees, like in a film, the furiously foaming Jewish lady Rebecca in the Vienna of 1908.

"Everything repeats in life!", the 42-year old Adolf Hitler murmurs and views with fright the appalled facial expression of his niece.

"Until now, she was my »Geli«, but whose »Geli« is she now?", this question shot hot as burning coal through his mind!

There she sits slumped into a heap on the sofa – completely petrified – her mouth wide open, as if she had just met the devil incarnate.

Even though she had felt strong, prepared for everything – this is something she really hadn't expected.

What a dreadful sight:
- on top, the half normal, flesh-coloured penis
- bottom left, the »crimson red cartilage extension«
- to the right, the »bloodless black lobe of skin«!

With this horrible sight, the normally formed testicles aren't really even noticeable.

»Geli« Maria Raubal, the articulate 22-year old »Fraeulein« from Linz, who normally isn't easily thrown, is completely devastated.

Of the young woman equipped with sparkling humour and with the gift to cheer people like Göring, Goebbels, Heß, there is nothing left to recognize. Dismayed and with eyes wide open she stares for seconds at the hanging, misshapen shape …

"Uncle »Alf«!",

she yells suddenly in full panic and storms out of the room.

Next morning Hitler's niece is gone! Mrs. Winter, the janitor's wife, says on being asked, »Geli« has ordered the chauffer to drive her to Berchtesgaden to »Haus Wachenfeld«.

Adolf Hitler, the good uncle, is furious!

A few hours later, the neighbours in Berchtesgaden hear the piercing cry of a young woman, followed by the long echo resounding from the nearby mountains.

"Mama, Mama!", with this cry »Geli« flings herself into her mother's arms.

The woman much experienced of life, recognizes immediately, that something terrible must have happened – pulls the totally exhausted daughter into the house and asks impatiently:

"»Geli«, child, what has happened?"

"It's Uncle »Alf« – the uncle!", she blurts out.

"It is so terrible! Uncle wanted to take me for »his wife« and showed me his »zippedeus«. Mama, you won't believe this, something so terrible, totally horrible you will never have seen!"

The daughter is exasperated – screams, cries, howls and curses with fury and shame – all at the same time. Her mother is incapable of consoling her daughter in that beautiful »Haus Wachenfeld« in Berchtesgaden.

The otherwise so strong woman slumps to a heap in her armchair:

"»Geli« Maria Raubal has suffered a nervous breakdown", is the sober diagnosis of the quickly consulted house doctor.

Next morning, at breakfast, the world seems to be in order once again.

"Well, my child, how do you feel?"

"Look, Mother, outside the panorama of the mountains of Berchtesgaden – what a sight in all its majesty. Just as the last traces of morning fog rise, light returns to the inside of me – everything becomes clear, like the new day."

"Child, don't talk in riddles. Have your fill and then explain to me how this thing with Uncle »Alf« is supposed to be going to continue."

"Yes, Mama, I don't have to strengthen myself first, I can go right ahead." – And daughter »Geli« begins to talk while her mother listens closely.

"You see, Mama", and the daughter is smiling once more, and has obviously regained her unshakable self-confidence.

"You see, Mother", she begins anew, and the smile has vanished. With a serious look on her face she slowly continues talking,

"after this restful night, everything is crystal clear – as firmly and immovable our mountains stand there, thus is my decision:

My future will take place without Herr Hitler! – »Geli« Maria Raubal will never be »Mrs. Chancellor of the Reich«!

Just as the morning mist has disappeared, so is also the veil gone, which brought forth my transfigured inside only shadowy – I never even recognized myself – so blinded was I.

Now I see everything more than clearly:
- Uncle »Alf« is such an egoist, beside whom I could never last.

- Has possibly that billy goat, that made his penis a real nightmare for every woman, something to do with his hatred on Jews and his devastating fury for everything and everyone who doesn't share his opinion? – Or haven't you, Mama, heard anything yet of the encounter of the nine-year old Uncle »Alf« with the billy goat of Leonding?

- The inner and outer virility of Herr Hitler are obviously so injured since the bite of that billy goat that he can react to the outside with hatred and murderous aggression only. The uncle is so evil, that there can be no intensification to the term »evil« any more.

As Uncle »Alf« had already as a nine-year old practiced violence on the billy goat by urinating into its mouth, the animal has taken revenge by the complete mutilation of his »zippedeus«:

>   Love does not necessarily generate more love,
>   but violence inevitably generates more violence!

With such a monster which Uncle »Alf« is now inside and outside – with such a creature I could never live together with – leave alone be in bed with him!

"But child", the mother throws in, and is startled by what »Geli« states.

"Please listen further, dear Mother, how I imagine my future to be without Uncle »Alf«:

To add to the misery, there is that woman, that Eva Braun. With that young thing, barely 19 years of age, Herr Hitler has been flirting around for months on end. Dates this »nymphet«, gives sweets and idolizes that apprentice of the Photoshop Hoffmann.

One gets the impression that Uncle »Alf« wants to cover up all his deficiencies with the youth of that bitch and with my youth as well.

I can already hear the cry of that »Photo tart«, when the super politician on his knees feigns his love for her, the gets up to let down his trousers and to present to her that »penis monster«!

Struck with horror, that young thing can do nothing but commit suicide: Take tons of pills or shoot herself!"

"But Child," the mother intervenes,

"think of everything you owe to Uncle »Alf«, and I, too. After all, he took me into »Haus Wachenfeld« as housekeeper – and that in times, when around 1928/29, we were all struck by the World Wide Economic Crisis, and in Germany and Austria the unemployment rate rose to immeasurable heights.

In those hard times the uncle hadn't forgotten his family, giving us work, bread and an exceedingly nice home!"

"That's just it, Mother, while you are slaving for the gentleman and he is trying to drag your daughter into his bed, the bastard whores around, and that all in public, with that little Braun.

I, too, have my informants; there are enough people who think that I, »Geli«, don't deserve that disgrace – and believe me, Mother, I'm informed of everything!

That adulterer has got more than one string to his bow – but believe me, Mother, that fire is just barely glowing and will never become a flaring fire of love! A »wise billy goat« doesn't even permit the faintest of glows. That abused animal from Leonding will again and again see to it, that the violator will cause fear and paralyzing shame to every newly appearing woman:

"The memory of a weak domesticated animal dominates that man who at some time strives to dominate whole peoples!"

"But child", the mother takes the word once more,

"don't sin against the Lord!" – And the daughter retaliates in a sharp tone never before heard towards her mother:

"The Lord didn't protect the billy goat from a pervert of a little boy – just like the Lord doesn't protect the in the meantime adult pervert from the revenge of that abused animal – that, dear Mother, is the justice of our God!"

"My dear little »Geli«, how am I to help you, you being so filled with hatred – and so unjust towards our great benefactor!"

But the daughter won't be talked out of the path she has taken, not even by the arguments of her mother – not the slightest bit and continues:

"The day before yesterday the Lord opened my eyes by means of an animal, dearest Mother. Was I occasionally blinded with raging jealousy of Eva Braun, I had within already forgiven the uncle, when he, really dearly and trustworthy, asked for my hand in marriage. But the Lord permitted me with the help of an animal to recognize my further path in life. A billy goat from rural Leonding showed me the way into my future with the irrefutable advice:

- ›**You, »Geli« Mara Raubal, will only have a future if you free yourself from the claws of that evil uncle.**
- **You have to get out of Prinzregentenplatz 16 in Munich – and that forever!**‹ "

"Child, »Geli«, Uncle Adolf won't let you go just like that. He isn't a man to let someone else have his toy. »Geli«, Child, the matter is extremely dangerous! Uncle Adolf, Goebbels, Göring and all the other won't permit it. The danger of you »spilling the beans« is much too great. They, the powerful, will all be afraid of you. After all, the NSPAP and their »Fuehrer« are standing on the threshold of power.

»Geli«, Child, your life is in extreme danger – you just know too much!"

"That's clear to me, Mama, and I will take precautions, do something for my own safety. It wasn't without reason that then

Goebbels gave me the nickname »Geli the intrepid«, when we were on holidays on the island of Heligoland, and I threw myself heroically into the freezing waters of the North Sea. Do you remember, Mother?

So listen, Mother, to come to an end: I will continue living in Uncle's house, until perhaps one day he will let me go in friendship, my loving »**prison warden**«.

Perhaps everything will shortly be resolved by itself, if he can, against all expectations, bring his new »flame«, Eva Braun, to finally flare up. A partner is essential to him, that he has already stated several times unmistakably. – And I, »Geli«, will then be of absolutely no importance to the gentleman – will perhaps be released in a roundabout way due to his new darling Eva.

And the campaign meetings, too, I will furthermore visit with Uncle »Alf«, and make the great men of his party laugh; that is something I am perfectly good at! And for that purpose, I don't even have to pretend, no, I was born with this talent – and even Uncle sometimes comes in the mood, when he then slaps his thighs with enthusiasm.

Despite all that, I will, as I have already said, take precautions for ma own security, in case the whole story escalates and the uncle won't free me.

In case of emergency I will then need a simple means to hold his own gun to that gentleman's head – very simple – I shall blackmail him with my intimate knowledge on him and his intrigues!

I do know so many things that can surely mess up Uncles career and spoil the power of the NSDAP. I shall write everything I know down to the last cent, and ask you, dear Mother, to keep all the documents safe for me."

The daughter embraces her mother lovingly and comes to the end:

"With you, dear Mother, all those highly charged documents will be absolutely safe. You will not betray me, you are my mother!"

And the confiding Miss »Geli« Maria Raubal, doesn't realize, that she has just pronounced her own death sentence!

Operation »Flight of the Swallow« (Schwalbenflug) –
The death sentence for »Geli« Raubal

Joseph Goebbels proved to be right!

He had already in the year 1925 judged the liaison between Adolf Hitler and »Geli« Raubal correctly, when everything began.

He, the academic with the subjects German Philology, The Classics and History, had in those days already come to Hitler's notice, when the latter made the acquaintance with the eloquent little man with the clubfoot.

Besides Adolf Hitler and perhaps Heß, nobody from the leading retinue liked this newcomer – the »brain dominated« as they called him.

During the time of his fortress imprisonment in the prison of Landsberg, the movement NSDAP was just on »dead«, because forbidden. The newly founding of the party wasn't achieved until the 27th of February 1925. Moreover, to the 9th of March 1925 it was Hitler forbidden to hold speeches in Bavaria. In addition, Hitler was from the 30th of April stateless, because Austria had, on his own application, discharged him from his nationality.

In those times of a new start, of upheaval of the »Hitler Movement«, which had then by no means established itself, Joseph Goebbels had bypassed the party ban pronounced after the »Hitler coup« in 1923.

Already in 1924 he founded as a cover organization, the »Local Branch of the National Socialist Freedom Movement of Greater Germany«. In addition he was engaged as clerk for the weekly paper »Voelkische Freiheit«.

In those days he was already Hitler's trustee and soon »informant« from the anti capitalistic wing of the NSDAP around Gregor and Otto Strasser, as well. Hitler was informed »to the cent« by Goebbels about everything this group was planning against the centralistic party leadership of Adolf Hitler – even though Goebbels himself originally belonged to this group.

A second man also appeared in 1925 in the sphere of influence of the »Fuehrer«: Martin Bormann, the son of a former military musician.

Though in the beginning not yet member of the NSDAP, he became member of the »Weimarer Frontbanner« led by Ernst Röm.

Typically enough, Bormann was, just like Goebbels, informant for Hitler, because the »Fuehrer« showed extreme interest in the development of the later powerful SA[24], the infamous »Brown Shirts« and especially in the doings of their »leader of the storm troops« Ernst Röm.

Already very early, Hitler, Goebbels and Bormann had formed a strong alliance, with Goebbels and Bormann pledging allegiance to their »Fuehrer« – to death and beyond!

To this alliance of the three, Heinrich Himmler joined in, who already very soon showed a talent for organization. Thus was created that »four-leaf-clover« which soon was to decide the fate of the German people and the entire world as a secret society of a sworn company.

These three were the only people to whom Hitler listened patiently – the only ones whom he secretly called »my friends«.

Also, theses three were the only men who had seen the »Fuehrer« undressed – he had revealed to them his physical affliction!

Thus it was the tactician Joseph Goebbels who immediately recognized the danger that emerged from »Geli« Raubal for the cause of the NSDAP and its »Fuehrer«.

As »Geli« had already become Hitler's ward at the age of 15, the family ties of the two became more and more firm. The relationship between the somewhat »rigid uncle« and the hearty and open »nature's child« from Linz became more and more close.

Even during his fortress imprisonment, »Geli« had visited her incarcerated uncle on June the 17th of 1924, together with her Mother and her brother Leo.

Following that, »Geli« really showed off by putting her personal closeness to her famous uncle in an exorbitant light. Especially before her class mates she boasted about the closeness to her family celebrity.

---

[24] *The »SA-Storm Troops«: A paramilitary combat organization of the NSDAP during the Weimar Republic, and later also becoming »Auxiliary Police« in the 3rd Reich.*

It hadn't escaped the attention of the true politician Goebbels how fast a man with the famous name of »Hitler« subdued to the charm of the so natural and bright girl.

Joseph Goebbels, the man with the small body but the huge intelligence – a talent as politician who could read all sorts of things into everything – realized at once, what danger this quick witted girl could bring their »Fuehrer« – yes, the entire »great cause«.

Quickly he noticed that from family ties there arose an acute and firm personal »bond«.

To him, the scrutinizing observer, the exceptionally gifted analyst with his innate eloquence, the growing intimacy of the relationship between »Geli« and Hitler became obvious, and which threatened to devour him and all his party comrades.

He always compared this with a ship on collision course. In the picture, Hitler's position was that of the captain who was taken, figuratively speaking, more and more off course by his pretty assistant. He lovingly neglected his sea charts, forgot his leadership towards the crew and threatened to let the ship run aground. The loss of ship and crew was to him the »writing on the wall« of a party coming to grief. The course set on seizure of power and the reshaping of the German Reich was severely at risk.

"Sooner or later that little Miss »Geli« Raubal will have all of us in her hands", so Goebbels.

"That is why already at the beginning of the journey, strong countermeasures have to be taken. It is inevitable to work out a **»rescue plan«** which will protect the »ship seizure of power«, its »Captain Adolf Hitler« and the »crew« recruited from the lines of the NSDAP", the far sighted Goebbels knows already in 1925!

So it was that already in those days, in case the romantic adventure of Adolf Hitler and the »nymphet« »Geli« Raubal should really one day go off course, the necessity arose to work out that plan quite early in time.

In this matter, Goebbels saw things quite clearly, because after Hitler's philosophy of partnership, the woman had to listen devoutly to what the man had to say and to enthusiastically applaud – no matter what the topic.

But Miss »Geli« didn't listen devoutly and didn't applaud either. On the contrary even at the age of 17 this young girl clearly what she thought of politics: namely nothing at all!

So, according to Goebbels, it was inevitably necessary to prepare that rescue plan and it was given the code word

»Flight of the Swallow«!

At this plan originally worked only Goebbels and Bormann until, as already stated, Himmler later joined them.

Because of the volatile nature of the topic nothing was put down in writing – not even cue words. There were, moreover, never any telephone calls. All arrangements were oral and not the slightest bit became known to any other person – only the inner core!

Now, in February 1931, the time had come!

The rescue plan »Flight of the Swallow« had now become highly topical, with Hitler beginning the dialog on the subject as follows:

"My dear Goebbels, without trustees no »Fuehrer« can prevail, and neither Alexander nor Napoleon and not even Frederic the Great were capable of it – and an »Adolf Hitler« least of all in these confused times.

Both of us, and, of course, Bormann and Himmler as well, want to shape the future of Germany that everything, simply everything is clearly regulated. To achieve this goal, it is absolutely inevitable to focus the absolute power on me, the »Fuehrer«.

Every man and every woman, too, exist furthermore only to obey:

To receive and to obey orders while travelling that path to our
1000-years Reich!

My dear Joseph Goebbels,

everyone dissenting has to be eliminated,
without any respect to persons!

Every man, and woman, too, who stands in opposition to our movement, all those who even only rebel, not support us, will end at the gallows, under the guillotine or in the hail of bullets of a firing squad. And if bullets are of too great a value, because we are waging a war, we will resort to gas. Only with an unrelenting severity and without mercy towards any of our enemies we will be able to prevail!

… That it is I, the »Fuehrer«, who is challenged to let deeds follow my words, is surely a strange twist of fate.

I am forced to par with the dearest I have. I am forced to destroy my »sweetheart«, sacrifice her for the cause – listen now, my friend Goebbels, what is coming over us.

Last night Miss Raubal's mother came to visit me and informed me:

›My daughter »Geli« has meticulously written everything she knows down – simply everything! With that she intends to blackmail the party and its »Fuehrer« to attain her freedom – that silly, pert »thing«!‹

To make the situation worse, »Geli« knows my genital mutilated by the billy goat, because I had shown it to her last month in a fit of weakness of romantic rapture for a common partnership.

Thus, to our rescue and to the rescue of my honour, the only possibility is to apply the rescue plan worked out in 1925!

Please, my friend Joseph Goebbels, do present to me once again the current version of the plan with the code word »Flight of the Swallow«!"

"»My Fuehrer«, Bormann and Himmler, too, totally agree with me in the matter of this tiresome business. There is absolutely no divergence between us. To tell you that, »My Fuehrer«, they have explicitly instructed me, and to convey their hearty greetings to you, »My Fuehrer«, too.

Concerning the matter I may state:

As a kind of »providence«, »My Fuehrer«, the friendship with Ferdinand Goldstein was given to you, him, whom you enrolled with party Number 49 in 1925, as the leader of the newly founded SS.

»Ferdi«, as you called your best friend in public, had been your chauffeur since 1921, and also an indispensable and intrepid combatant in all political meeting brawls with the communists.

»Ferdi« also accompanied you to your incarceration on »Fortress Landsberg«, even had to stay there longer than you – your true and only bosom buddy!

Already very early, with your consent, we instructed Ferdinand Goldstein to court Miss »Geli« Raubal – and Miss

Raubal reciprocated the advances of that handsome, guitar playing gentleman.

In this, the matter of the heart we faked, everything went like a clockwork!

Though we did have concerns in the beginning, that Miss »Geli«, because of her so self confident appearance, couldn't perhaps be seduced – very unusual for a young girl that already has own opinions to all sorts of things and puts them in words, too, – this proved to be groundless.

This trait of character she already displayed when she then, with her final-year class »8A« and the teachers of History, Prof. Hermann Toppa and of German, Michael Watschinger, came to visit you, »My Fuehrer«.

Though it was still commendable, having helped to plan the eight-day journey to Munich at the end of her school days and as a crowning final suggested a visit to »Austria's son« Adolf Hitler, her famous relative, it wasn't at all commendable that she described her relationship to you, »My Fuehrer« as follows:

›Adolf Hitler to me is merely the »dear uncle« and only coincidentally politician. I myself am a totally apolitical woman!‹

›If only you would have remained silent‹, my teacher used to say when we were as pert as Miss »Geli«!

I was even then of the opinion, that someone who makes such remarks in public, could only with difficulty become »Mrs. Chancellor of the Reich«.

And this example shows with emphasis how far sighted and necessary, »My Fuehrer«, your order was already in 1925, to begin defensive measures in the sense of »Flight of the Swallow«.

In addition, the passing of the school-leaving exam on the 24th of June in 1927, amidst boys only, at the Academic College of Linz, indicated that an extremely difficult to guide person would be entering the private life of the »Fuehrer«!

Ferdinand Goldstein had nearly daily contact with Miss Raubal, because in his position as a chauffeur, he drove the entire »Hitler Company« to all private picnics and to their campaign meetings. He thus had known Miss »Geli« for years and played his part as admirer very convincing. Perhaps there was a bit of liking to go with it. Otherwise Ferdinand Goldstein didn't have to make an effort concerning the female sex – women's' hearts simply came his way easily.

I, Goebbels, can only express my greatest respect, after years of observation, of »Ferdi's« behavior, because didn't forget once, that he was merely fulfilling a task, and that the woman he had to take care of, belonged to his »Fuehrer«.

Here your far-sightedness shows, »My Fuehrer«, that besides Bormann, Himmler and myself as well, you let us swear obedience until and beyond death, with the result:

1.   Ferdinand Goldstein manages to bring Miss »Geli« to like him as a man – 1926 it actually turns to love.

2.   »Ferdi« talked publicly to other people and to me, even in the presence of a news paper journalist. He complains about his unhappy love which he expects will never be tolerated by you as her guardian.

3.   Beginning of 1927 Goldstein asks »Geli« to become his wife – »Geli« consents and they become engaged.

4.   At Christmas 1927 Goldstein asks you, the guardian, for your niece's hand in marriage.

5.   You, »My Fuehrer«, reject the proposal and cause a terribly loud scene in all public – played especially well and convincing by a worried guardian. My admiration for you, »My Fuehrer« for the absolutely strong and credible acting performance!

Everyone in the audience, especially the press, had to assume, that not much was missing until you swung the riding whip against the completely dumbfounded man ready to marry. With him, »Ferdi«, great talent for acting could be observed. No other could have displayed more convincing fear and horror in the face of the threatening whip. I can still see the eyes wide open and filled with fear!

6.   You as the guardian, »My Fuehrer« ordered a two-years waiting period for the 31-year old Goldstein and your 19-year old ward until marriage.

7.   »Geli« writes glowing love letters to her Ferdinand.

8. You, as »Fuehrer« of the NSDAP terminate Ferdinand Goldstein's job as a chauffeur and withdraw all party posts, exile him from your vicinity.

9. For the time being there is no further feigned break between the two of you.

10. I and my half-sister go on holidays with »Geli« and her mother to the island of Heligoland in 1928.

   My comment based on intensive observation during that time: Ferdinand Goldstein's name has already been written off his fiancées list and was forgotten, too.

11. »Geli« Maria Raubal, at the beginning of 1928, advances to become steady companion of her famous uncle, enchants the entire »circle« around you, »My Fuehrer«, with her lovable and natural manner.

12. Goldstein appeals against the dismissal without notice decreed by you and sues the NSDAP as his employer. He wins before the industrial tribunal and is awarded compensation.

Nobody besides us knows that this suit was arranged by us as well. Particularly no one knows, that the compensation Mr. Goldstein received was immediately paid back to us by him, namely to a secret account of the NSDAP.

Ferdinand Goldstein, the sacked party member, who, for everyone publicly recognizable, wanted to snatch from you, Adolf Hitler, his girl, who is wildly lashing out in all directions against his own party – Ferdinand Goldstein, party member No. 49, who is delivering arguments to the communists and social democrats against his own friends in the NSDAP, and who has especially turned against his bosom buddy, namely you our »Fuehrer« – that Ferdinand Goldstein has all of a sudden turned from a bosom buddy to an enemy, and that for all the public to see!

Thereby Ferdinand Goldstein is the ideal executor of our plan with the code word »Flight of the Swallow«!

So »Ferdi« is going to carry it out!

He will silence that irksome and having developed to a danger »Geli« Maria Raubal!

He shall end the life of that pert miss!

No one will imagine Ferdinand Goldstein to have been the perpetrator, he, the by you, Adolf Hitler, humiliated looser in the quest for the favour of »Geli« Raubal.

Now I may put forward a few technical details:

Long-term the action is intended for the 18th of September 1931, when you, »My Fuehrer«, are going to the mass rally in Hamburg.

You, »My Fuehrer« will probably be reached by the message of the death of your ward somewhere near Nuremberg. You will then immediately turn around and proceed at excessive speed back to Munich.

The police have already been instructed to issue your driver with a ticket for speeding.

With that, the so very important question of the alibi for the »Fuehrer« is solved – as always, »The police your friend and helper!«

The weapon involved will be your pistol, »My Fuehrer«, a Walter caliber 6.35 mm, which lies, as always, in the unlocked drawer in your home, in the room immediately next to the one of Miss Raubal.

The janitor couple is using your absence to do some shopping. The big house on Prinzregentenplatz 16 is empty – Miss »Geli« Raubal is alone at home!

Ferdinand Goldstein, too, takes advantage of the absence of his former employer. He will visit Miss Raubal in the company of her mother.

Miss »Geli« will surely let him and her mother into the house, and be happy about the unexpected arrival of her former fiancé, because neither of them has completely severed the ties, as we know for sure.

The authorized version of the particulars of the crime on the next day will be:

›**Adolf Hitler's niece, Miss »Geli« Maria Raubal, has committed suicide by taking her life with the gun of her guardian!**‹

You, »My Fuehrer«, will later state, that before your departure to Hamburg, to have had a small disagreement of opinion with your ward – it was about a journey of Miss »Geli« to Vienna, planned by her.

The Couple Winter, too, will report of this dispute to the police, because the words of the »Fuehrer« could hardly not be heard due to a certain volume. Thus you will, »My Fuehrer«, admit to something that is well known anyhow.

You, »My Fuehrer«, will the react with dismay and words something like:

- ›Whatever may have gone on in that child?‹
- ›Why is she causing me such sorrow?‹
- ›The way in which our loved by everyone has left us, I, the uncle, feel to be horrifying, absolutely incomprehensible – we have no explanation whatsoever for this act!‹

The police will quickly close the case »Suicide of Miss Angelika Maria Raubal«, and you, »My Fuehrer« can calmly and as planned go to the mass rally in Hamburg.

The entire sad matter around the death of Miss Raubal is absolutely »watertight« – even communists and social democrats can do nothing but spread lies – their stories will soon come to nothing, because it is something completely »plucked out of the air« – without any weight and containing no trace of truth!

After the crime Ferdinand Goldstein disappears from public focus, disappears from the face of the earth and goes underground!

Goldstein can, yes, he must, because of his services to us, take part in our cause again. Also nothing stands in the way of a private reconciliation with you, his bosom buddy Adolf Hitler. We could then by all means celebrate the new »closing of ranks« effectively in public.

The Party and its »Fuehrer« never forget services rendered in loyalty and unselfishness, which in the case of Ferdinand Goldstein went as far as self-denial, entirely according to the oath by which we are bound »until death and beyond«.

Goldstein will be safe from his »bloodhounds« as long as he lives. That we can already now, seven months before the actual event, take for granted, because the defence plan »Flight of the Swallow« is so perfect, that our friend »Ferdi« can follow his family duties totally relaxed for all future. He can then find time to produce a new Aryan generation. He has already got a new love: A strapping super blonde German girl with deep-blue eyes and long plaits, who I already had the opportunity to look at delightedly.

I now close my lecture and thank you, »My Fuehrer« for the patience rendered."

The Murderers are coming –
The end of Hitler's niece »Geli«

»Knock, knock, knock« – it knocks three times on the door of the corner room on the second floor of the house on Prinzregentenplatz 16 in Munich.

It is the 18th of September 1931, 5 p.m.

Outside the leaves are beginning to fall – autumn is on its way.

»Knock, knock, knock – knock«, now there are four knocks on the door and a bit louder, too.

From the in side there comes the somewhat astonished voice of Angela Raubal, affectionately called »Geli« by everyone:

"Mrs. Winter, is that your? Didn't you want to go shopping with your husband?"

"No, my child, it's me, your mother, and I have brought along a very dear person, someone you surely haven't forgotten – a surprise."

"Wait, Mother, I'll open up – I've got everything barricaded – one can never know, in this big house and with the restless times. Wait, Mother, I've nearly got it", and one hears the sound of several locks, padlocks probably, too, in which keys are turned and bolts are turned up. Even the rustling of a steel chain can be heard.

"There, Mother", and the heavy wooden door swings open.

"»Ferdi«, my beloved Ferdinand, that's what I call a real surprise", – and she throws herself into the arms of »Handsome Ferdinand«, as he is called in the world of the ladies, and hugs him lovingly, in the course of which kisses are even given on the mouth.

„»Geli« hasn't got any time for her mother, and her mother asks while looking examining into her daughter's eyes:

"Well, Child, do I see a few tears of joy there? I thought I'd visit you while Uncle »Alf« in to the mass rally in Hamburg and I just took »Ferdi« along."

In the meantime »Ferdi« has taken a seat in the armchair and placed a small bunch of flowers and a little box of chocolates on the table.

Ferdinand Goldstein, the used to be fiancé of Miss Raubal smiles. And thus looking at him in his four-coloured woodcutter shirt – with open collar, wide combat trousers, silk lumber jacket and shining high boots as well as his inimitable smile on his face with the small moustache, one might well say without exaggeration: »smart lad«!

When he, with his immaculate physique and his clear eyes beams at the girls, then one understands why all women's hearts simply fly to him – that dark haired man – more the Mediterranean type.

»Geli's« little girly heart, too, in those days soon was smitten with the charm of this lady-killer.

"But that was so long ago!", »Geli« softly says to herself, a bit like in a dream,

"already so infinitely long ago!", she adds for herself.

"But a beautiful time it was, when I loved Ferdinand – my first great love!", this thought goes through her head within seconds.

But then the dream of a lost love leaves her as quickly as she began to dream it and she asks:

"What's on the minds of both of you, or is your visit just a kind of courtesy call – cheering up of the little lonesome »Geli« – well, never mind, I'm really happy to see you.

There, Mama, there's still some tea on the table, would you please serve Ferdinand some? You know your way around. I'll go to the bathroom in the meantime to freshen up a bit – I've been sleeping as you can see – sorry for the mess."

And »Geli« quickly leaves the wonderfully furnished room with the unmade single bed made of precious wood.

She goes into the bathroom which she and her Uncle »Alf« both use in common. The huge flat of the upcoming »Fuehrer« of the Germans and the corner room of his niece are situated close together.

For a long time already though, the young lady had wished for a bathroom of her own.

Recently everything has changed. When the uncle and his niece meet in the bathroom, the uncle just »looks through her« – doesn't notice her at all – just as if she weren't there.

In former days the mood was exuberant, and the uncle beamed at the sight of his niece – even cracked a joke now and then.

Everything has changed since »that day«!

Since that day, when during their first intimate meeting with the »Fuehrer« she had to perceive his physical ailment, since the uncle's account of the shame of Leonding, she detests the »Fuehrer« of that mighty party. Her disgust, yes, her horror has changed her thoughts and mind. If there was once affection of a warm, tender heart of a girl, now everything has turned cold. Soliloquizing and in her thoughts she described this heart as having turned to stone. She doesn't feel anything anymore for her uncle.

»Geli« comes back out of the bath, beams at Ferdinand and briefly looks at her mother, too, who has seated herself in the second armchair.

"An austere, big, strong woman the mother is", it comes to »Geli« – and she finds the thought on her mother at this moment rather inappropriate, more so as her mother isn't standing but sitting.

It's different with Ferdinand, »Ferdi«, – still the »charmer« from back then: »A first class heartbreaker«!

»Geli« felt a bit of a heart-warming sensation, thinking how the »smart Ferdinand« day by day and bit by bit conquered small pieces of her heart: Especially on those balmy evenings, when they were sitting, after the picnic with Uncle »Alf«, out in the open.

When then the »most handsome chauffeur in all of Germany«, as »Geli« used to rave, took his guitar to conjure Irish folk songs from it, the little miss from Linz just melted away – her heart was irretrievably lost!

"Now, my dears", »Geli« ends the mind's flashback on the happiest time of her young life.

"I am so happy", she beams at her guests.

While she is pouring herself a cup of tea, too, she lounges around a bit on the sofa, where she, in the meantime, has taken a seat – and »Geli« Raubal seems quite satisfied, actually happy in the »circle of her loved ones«.

"My child", the mother begins, and »Geli« is rather astonished how serious both of the others have suddenly become.

"Like hewn in stone Mother's face seems … a proper change of mood from »up one minute to down to the next«", »Geli« thinks, looking at the two people from the other side of the coffee table.

"My child", the mother begins once more, and one notices, that talking is not one of her strong points. That was one of the reasons why her daughter had to absolutely go to high school and take her »Matura«[25]. The child was to have better opportunities than her mother resulting from a better school education, who always fed the family with her hands' work.

"My dear, beloved child", the mother starts off for a third time.

Meanwhile Ferdinand Goldstein makes really sad face while casting down his eyes and staring at the table surface. His hands are folded and resting in his lap.

"Whatever is the matter with the two of you, why the unexpected change of mood – I thought you were happy to see your little »Geli« again!"

"My more than everything beloved child", the mother begins a fourth time,

"»Ferdi« and I have a very difficult and possibly very sad task to fulfill. But before that we want to convey the kindest of regards from Uncle »Alf«. We are to ask you, my child, how you imagine your future to become."

"So you are here to act on his behalf – not a friendly visit after all, so we might as well have a »general cleanout«, and here now the answer", »Geli« states annoyed, and in her voice there are overtones of great disappoint:

"I have often begged him to let me go,

I want my freedom!",

»Geli« shouts out – beside herself with rage.

---

[25] *»Matura« (German: Abitur): Austrian Certificate of Secondary Education / High School Leaving Certificate. Also called Matriculation Certificate.*

"That rogue won't free me! He, my »prison warden« keeps me under lock and key, keeps me from the eyes of the public. The fellow is obviously afraid of me!

As he won't let me go voluntarily, I'm going to fight for my freedom. I do know such a lot about the party and of him personally as well, that if I were to »talk« the whole of the Nazi movement would have had it.

To gain my freedom I will blackmail the great Mr. Hitler and his party, the NSDAP!

You, »Ferdi« once showed how it is to be done. You sued the NSDAP and appealed against your dismissal without notice. You won before the court of arbitration and even secured yourself compensation. Just as you, Ferdinand Goldstein, have won, I am going to prevail too!

I have written down everything and kept it safe with Mama in »Haus Wachenfeld«! I know a lot more about this »clean outfit« than any of you can imagine.

I was often present, when that »Mr. Clean Hitler« fiddled with the others – with the capital, too, the people with money. The »gentleman« then used to show off his »jewel«, the clever Miss »Geli«. And I silly, conceited goose was happy every time to support the criminal intrigues of our Uncle »Alfi« by cheering up bank fat cats and company bosses!"

»Geli« pauses a bit, but both the listeners suspect that Miss Raubal has put in the break only to create tension, because it is obvious that she wants to let loose some more … and indeed, without any further transition she immediately »spills the beans«.

"Just one sole matter, a very personal thing, will sweep away that whole insincere rabble:

As both of you know, and you, »Ferdi« aren't member of the SS without reason – as both of you know, already now, in 1931, Heinrich Himmler is working on a euthanasia project, even though the NSDAP hasn't got the absolute majority yet.

All life which doesn't meet up with the »standard« to 100 percent shall be exterminated and hindered from fathering further »unworthy« life. Belonging to this category are the Jews, everyone mentally ill, but all persons with severe physical deficiencies as well.

The human being of the future is, the master race, to be blond, has a light skin and is sane in the head and at the body!

What do both of you, my dears, think if the press, the communists, the social democrats, but all loyal followers of the NSDAP, too, get to know, that the leader of the whole movement is a »branded one«, to whom the new euthanasia laws which he himself dew up, apply to 100 percent!

What is your opinion, my dears, if it becomes public that the reproductive organ of the role model of millions consists of three parts:

- a little piece of »pink tail«
- a »crimson red cartilage extension«
- and a »lobe of skin void of blood«!

The role model of millions is himself a terrible cripple – equipped with a »penis range« with which he couldn't reproduce even if he wanted to!

A terrible nightmare that has absolutely nothing to do with the penis of an »Aryan Man«!

That »nightmare« is, because of its abnormal shape, in no way capable of penetrating the womb of a woman!

An Aryan woman, as described by the party and raised as a figurehead, give in to such a man. Even if she, overcoming her disgust, could, this Aryan, defying any description of the term, Mister Hitler would not be capable of carrying out any sexual intercourse. He is, to state it clearly, an »impotent imposter«.

»How disgusting, what scum!«"

And »Geli« punches the tabletop with her little fist – crimson red in the face with anger.

Her mother has put her head in both of her hands and supports her arms on the table.

White as a sheet she stares in disbelief at her daughter.

She can't say anything – to her ears »Geli's« story is so frightening, that even if her intellect would permit it, she wouldn't be capable of uttering a single word. Her voice chords are paralyzed, that she feels quite clearly.

Thus she sits motionless for at least a whole minute, holding the big shopping bag, from which the handles dangle to the floor, on her knees and under her arms.

On gets the impression that there is something in there she has to protect, because she presses it, as for security, with her belly against the tabletop.

Ferdinand Goldstein, too, seems totally speechless. He is sitting like an old man, slumped in a heap in his armchair. His shoulders turned to the front he has now stretched out both arms, placing his folded hands on the table.

Ferdinand Goldstein makes the impression, as if the whole matter were none of his business – keeps looking down on his folded hands just as if they were of such interest that one had to stare at them for minutes.

»Geli« looks closely at the two people on the other side of the table and can't grasp, why her speech has so distressed her loved ones: Her own mother incapable of even a single word, and the former fiancé lost in thought – probably praying.

»Geli« is now sure that Goldstein is praying, which thoroughly astonishes her, because »Ferdi« had often scorned God and Jesus in her presence.

"Those two are for weaklings only. I, on the other hand, grab the leg of a chair and help myself!", he used to say sounding very convinced of himself.

"Strange, now »Ferdi« is praying", »Geli« assesses for herself once again – to her, a completely new and totally inexplicable trait. Up to now she was actually convinced to know her former fiancé quite well, and she listens to him murmuring about God and Jesus. And the names Adolf Hitler and »Geli« come across his lips.

Ten minutes in total silence have passed, accompanied only by the soft murmuring of Goldstein.

Then the mother opens the zipper of the huge shopping bag, takes a big stack of papers from it and places it with a slapping noise on the smooth, wooden tabletop.

The stack is neatly stitched together with decorative tape.

On the top overlay there is written in big printed letters:

>>Angela Maria Raubal, born on
July 4th of 1908 in Linz, Austria,

noted down in hand writing
In September of the year 1931 in Munich«

The mother again reaches into the huge shopping bag, slams a pair of scissors, causing a loud noise, on the tale and in addition a closely written sheet of deckle-edge paper and an oversized, important looking pen.

The mother now stands up, puts herself in a straight upright position and points with the index finger of her right hand first on the stack of paper. Now that she is standing upright, one can actually see how big and how strong she really is.

Meanwhile Ferdinand Goldstein is still murmuring – sitting totally listless slumped in his armchair. Again the words God, Jesus, Adolf and »Geli« can be heard – now very much more clearly than before.

The mother puts on an »official expression« and begins to talk:

"»Geli« Raubal, Daughter, now listen very carefully to what your mother has to say to you."

Her voice until now very calm, soft and friendly has now become unusually sharp, forceful.

The mother continues, her facial expression nearly petrified:

"»Geli« Maria Raubal, Daughter, now take the big pair of scissors and cut the stack of papers, which you wrote, into small parts, and the scrap pieces into tiny little bits which then nobody will be able to read. Following that, »Ferdi« and I will collect all the snippets and safely burn them in the stove.

After you have torn up everything to the smallest possible, you will sign this attached document with your own hand, and Ferdinand and I will sign it as witnesses with date and Christian- and Family name.

Hear the very last family and friendship chance Uncle »Alf« is conceding to you. I will now read the text out to you:

›I, Angela Maria Raubal, called »Geli«. Born on the 4th of June 1908 in Linz, Austria, herewith declare before God and the two witnesses present in lieu of an oath:

I will never pass any information from the life and the sphere of the NSDAP and its »Fuehrer« Adolf Hitler to any other person or institution.

This is valid for all knowledge gained by me from the factual and personal environment. That applies also to all future knowledge, no matter in what way I will have gained it.

I will never leave my uncle Adolf Hitler, and not further ask him for my »so called freedom«.

I am now prepared to obediently serve the NSDAP and its »Fuehrer«, as long as I may live, until death.

This holy oath I swear as devout Christian, before God, our Lord Jesus and Mother Maria.‹

Signed personally on the 18th of September 1931 in Munich.

....
(Angela Maria »Geli« Raubal)

....
(Ferdinand Goldstein)   · The witnesses ·

....
(Angela Raubal, nee´ Hitler)

There is absolute silence in that homely room, because Ferdinand Goldstein, too, has finished his murmured prayers. The mother sits down in her armchair once again – she appears totally exhausted.

All of a sudden »Geli« jumps to her feet, reaches for her uncle's document written on deckle-edge paper and tears it up so forcefully that one could well assume that her fury would have enabled her to tear up a thick telephone book. The bits and pieces of the document she throws into the faces of her mother and Goldstein. The thick pen lands with a clatter in the far left corner of the room.

Then she shouts in an overturning voice:

"Traitors!",

while glaring full of hatred at the two people.

»Geli« briefly starts in fright, just as if an important thought just hit her. She grabs the stack of papers that she had written and which weighs one and a half kilos, off the table and presses it to her chest with both hands, just as if she had to protect it from some »imaginary power«. She slumps down deeply into her sofa and begins to cry heartrendingly.

All of a sudden there comes movement into Ferdinand Goldstein, too. With his hands folded in his lap her and »Geli's« mother rise simultaneously.

Both of then sadly look at the slumped down »child of man«, but merely for seconds, and then the mother once more reaches into the big shopping bag:

- with her left hand she holds the handle of the bag,
- with her right hand she »conjures« out a large pistol – the uncle's weapon, a Walther
- and with a clearly audible bang places it on the wooden table top.

"There, Angela Raubal, take the weapon and do the only thing that is left for you to do", the mother hisses.

"You are bringing the whole »Movement«, for which millions have worked devotedly and under threat of life, into trouble. You, Maria »Geli« Raubal have betrayed those millions, the party, their »Fuehrer«, as well as Ferdinand Goldstein and even your own mother.

I carried you under my heart, had born you in pain and raised lovingly. You, my only daughter, will always be my child. The uncle in his generosity has offered you a last chance – and you didn't take advantage of it.

You could have made up for everything in a matter of seconds! The millions of followers, the party, their »Fuehrer« and you, too, my child would once again have been safe. Everything could again be as if nothing had happened.

But you, my daughter are stubborn, thick- headed and headstrong as always! Moreover, a new trait is added »stupidity« – for a high school student with high-sounding ambitions, very unusual.

Now, my child, your former fiancé and your mother bid you farewell!

In front of you there lies the well known to you Uncle »Alf's« weapon – it is loaded and cocked. You are experienced in shooting and you know the uncle's weapon from the shooting range. Aim at the heart – there!", and points to her own one with her index finger of the right hand.

"Aim at your heart. A woman doesn't shoot herself in the head – and it doesn't hurt – completely painless!

I will see you in heaven, »Geli«, my child. From now you have half an hour to do it – exactly 30 minutes!”

“I, too, say »see you in heaven«, dearest »Geli«”, »Ferdi« now feels obliged to take the word as well.

The mother and Ferdinand Goldstein turn around and leave the room.

The door falls shut – and »Geli« is alone:

- with the stack of incriminating evidence
- her own thoughts
- the pistol of her uncle.

And »Geli« the clever girl is not quite as stupid as her mother thinks. The »Fuehrer« Adolf Hitler’s niece has understood. She knows, that this is the end for her.

… Exactly 30 minutes have passed.

As no shot broke the silence, »Ferdi« and the mother enter the room again.

“Mama, Mama”, the young woman whimpers,

“I can’t do it, Mama – help me!”

And »Geli« puts her mother’s hand on her own trembling little hand and on the weapon.

“Child”, the mother says, takes the weapon and also the stack of papers from »Geli’s« chest – puts both on the table.

“Child, are there any more papers – perhaps hidden?”

“Of course I still have some, but where they are I won’t tell”, »Geli« defiantly blurts out. And the young woman sits up straight as an arrow on her position on the sofa.

»Geli’s« mother and Ferdinand Goldstein briefly look at each other. As on an agreed sign, the big woman leaves the room, pulling the door shut behind her with such force that there is a crash.

Nor Ferdinand Goldstein walks around the table directly towards where »Geli« is sitting, walks up close to her and says in his sonorous voice:

“»Geli«, don’t make it any more difficult for us than it already is. Where are your other documents?”

"Now I won't say anything anymore. May people get to know after me what is going on here. Uncle…"

She wants to continue talking, but doesn't get any further than »Uncle«, because then there is a short, hard bang. »Geli's« little nose immediately swells up and blood begins to drip.

The in so many political brawls experienced SS-thug has suddenly hit »Geli« in the face with the outer edge of his fist and brutally broken her nose.

There is nothing left of the »seducer of ladies«, the smiling »charmer«: His face has turned into a stone hard grimace – the eyes alone could kill. … Then without any warning the second blow, now with his closed fist directly to »Geli's« chest!

»Geli« cries out with pain and collapses.

The locally well known SS-thug pulls the girl to her feet by her blouse striking her with his hands left and right on her cheeks and on her ears – resulting in »Geli's« repeated collapse on the sofa.

With eyes closed tightly she squints up at her former admirer and softly utters:

"You, too, are a pig – the great disappointment of my life! And even my mother is unfathomable bad: Doesn't take any steps against the death of her daughter by that gang of murderers."

"You are right again, stupid bitch. I am really bad. I am, however, only bad when it is against rabble – to which you belong – that wants to harm my beloved »Fuehrer« and our »holy cause«.

In that case my loyalty to »Fuehrer« and party win – sworn by a »holy oath«.

So now listen, »Geli« Raubal, just how bad I can get when stupidity and impertinence, like you are showing, threaten our beloved »Fuehrer«:

- Right from the beginning our love was faked.
- I played the admirer on order of the party-like in a film.
- love-stricken Miss »Geli« was cheated real proper!

Because one thing we did realize quite early: We imagined, that one day you could, with your impudent big mouth, endanger our »holy cause«!

Already in 1925, that is six years ago, it became clear to all of us, that it could well become inevitable , that one day Ferdinand

Goldstein, your »admirer«, would have to send you to the »happy hunting grounds« – if that Miss Raubal really posed a danger.

That situation has now occurred and everything had long been planned. Tomorrow, no one in the whole world will in any way suspect, that he, the from the NSDAP dismissed »Ferdi« is the culprit!"

"Mama, Mama – come", the daughter calls her mother for a the last time,

"help me, quickly, take this monster from me! Free me from this swine and from the imposter that wants to become the »Fuehrer« of all Germans! Let me have a good laugh for a last time about these two wimps for the last few minutes that I've got left – they shall burn in hell forever!

About you, Ferdinand Goldstein, even your own party comrades are cracking jokes:

**›Ferdinand Goldstein the Aryan and so courageous, too,
still by name and all his looks, simply just a Jew.‹**

How can anyone with jet-black hair and beard – of who it is said that he himself is a Jew – how can anyone be so conflicting that he goes hunting for his own »companions in faith«, together with his SS-henchmen?

Obviously there are people

- with a conscience
- without any conscience
- and people with a two-fold conscience, like Ferdinand Goldstein!

Farewell, my »love«, the devil shall take you!

God will surely help you on your way to hell, just as he will now help me, through your hands, to get to heaven.

How happy I am, the little girl from Linz:
In a few minutes I will see
My Lord Jesus Christ and his Mother Maria –
Only now will my life become really beautiful!"

"Just go outside, Angela", Ferdinand Goldstein meanwhile says in a calm voice to »Geli's« mother, who appeared once again hearing »Geli's« cries of pain,

"I'll help the »child« along", and the mother isn't deign to look at her daughter, turns around, walks through the door and closes it behind her – this time softly!

Now everything happens really quickly:

Ferdinand Goldstein drags »Geli« to the centre of the room, sands her on her feet, reaches for the pistol and shoots the young woman close beneath her heart into her lungs.

He puts the girl face down on the floor so that she comes to lie on her chest and belly. Then the murderer bends down to her, puts is mouth to »Geli's« ear and whispers clearly audible to her:

"That for the »wimps«, and should my bosom buddy Adolf and I one day burn in hell for our »holy cause« – well, so be it.

But you floozy, who has always looked down full of pity on our »movement«, you stuck-up »high school chuck« from Linz, shall struggle another twenty hours for your life before death relieves you.

I know where to shoot so that it really hurts and that it takes a really long time.

Have a nice journey on your way to heaven!"

He walks over to the bed, because the flitting gaze of the dying woman, who once more had straightened up slightly, was suspiciously long directed on the resting place. He walks there, and pulls from under the mattress four more stacks of incriminating material all closely written by »Geli« Raubal. Triumphantly he waves it in the air, full of happiness, as if he had just performed a great feat. To »Geli's« mother who on hearing the shot had again entered the room, he says:

"Sooner or later they all talk!" and Ferdinand Goldstein seem rather satisfied.

Having tidied up the room, put the pistol in »Geli's« hand and stowed away all the papers in the big shopping bag, the »mother« and the former »darling« of »Geli« Raubal look at one another smiling and in self satisfaction.

They have even thought of the tea cups. Nothing, absolutely nothing, indicates that the niece of the »Fuehrer« had two visitors.

While »Geli« is lying on the floor, wheezing loudly and dying of suffocation, the two murderers disappear unnoticed.

That »Geli« Raubal's murderers will stay undiscovered for the rest of their lives, the ingenious accomplices of Adolf Hitler had made sure:

Joseph Goebbels, Heinrich Himmler and Martin Bormann, the dictator's henchmen, have done an excellent job. Their defence plan with the code word »Flight of the Swallow« was, in their opinion, a complete success!

The Escalation of »Evil« –
The highly developed people of the »Toranians« in the Andromeda galaxy anticipate the danger of a 3rd World War on the Earth of humans in 1944/45

..... After theses horrible happenings, Immo and his father look at one another aghast. The father, however, the four-star general on the planet of »Tora« gets a grip on himself more quickly than Immo is able to.

"Well, my Son, now you are surprised what types of people you meet in the course of your history studies. With Adolf Hitler from the species »Humans« we did, however, choose something special – without show of conscience he murders little »Geli« and will otherwise as well, stop at nothing.

He is a man who has only one sole goal:

»The achievement of absolute power«!

That goal he pursues with his virtually iron will and won't be dissuaded despite suffering knockbacks.

He wants to achieve absolute power in Germany by forcing all Germans under the dictatorship of one person only – himself!

The »German« wants to be »someone« once again after the disgraceful defeat of the World War in 1918. And »the Germans« have by no means forgotten how the British and French oppressed them with the dictated Peace of Versailles.

›That Adolf Hitler will change everything, and very soon we will be the »Master-race« once more, and no longer feel like slaves to the French!‹, so it was spoken in all parts of Germany, but also in Austria.

The murder of »Geli« Raubal shows, with which cruel strategy and determination this »new Fuehrer« pursues his goal. And this »New Redeemer« has success with the people, success beyond description!

Especially the young people already have got a stiff arm from all that stretching towards the sky and a croaky voice from all that ›Heil Hitler‹ screaming!

We »Toranians« have, in all of our million years of development, never brought forth a man as »evil« as the creature by the Name of Adolf Hitler.

The question, why we »Toranians« are so very interested in the events happening on Earth I, has already been answered, when one thinks of it, that once we ourselves had destroyed that home planet by wars, disasters and overexploitation of natural resources.

The settlement of our successors, the humans, was to supply on the basis of a large-scale test, insights if this species is able to learn and to build a golden future with their experience gained.

The summary of our observations on that Mr. Hitler and his huge row of supporters, lets us fear that not only does one not learn, but on the contrary, stumble within a time span of merely 200,000 years like lemmings into the apocalypse of doom – unconscious and senseless.

That danger would, indeed, have been at hand, if Hitler had drawn more peoples into the vortex of war. Especially the seduction of the million-strong peoples of the Islam could have escalated to a world-wide extensive fire of war.

Hitler's war in West, South, East and North would have, together with the Japanese in Far East in connection with fanaticism instilled into over 100 millions of Muslims, kindled a dangerous global »fire«.

This is an assessment that Hitler agrees to himself at the end of his life, by stating that he should have brought about the global war even more determined and more maliciously than he already had. Thus one can read word for word with Joachim Fest, the famous author from Earth I, in his Hitler biography:

›Looking at the events sober-minded and void of sentimentality, I must admit that my unchangeable friendship towards Italy and to

the Duce can be put into the account of my mistakes. Indeed, one can say that our alliance with Italy has served our enemies more than ourselves ... and it will contribute in the end – unless the victory shall still be ours eventually – to us losing the war...

*The Italian ally has inhibited us nearly everywhere. He has, for instance, prevented us from practicing a **revolutionary policy** in Northern Africa..., because our Islamic friends suddenly viewed us as voluntary or involuntary accomplices of their oppressors ... the memory of the barbaric retaliatory attacks against the **Senoussi** was still in their minds. [...] There was the opportunity of great politics towards Islam. It was missed – like a lot of other things we neglected because of our fidelity to the Italian alliance...*

On the side of the military it is hardly any better. Italy's entry into the war nearly immediately gave first victories to or opponents and enabled Churchill to inspire new courage in his fellow countrymen and in all anglophiles around the world. Though the Italians had already proven themselves incapable to hold Abyssinia and the Cyrenaica, they had the audacity to throw themselves into the absolutely senseless war with Greece, without as much as asking us or even rendering any kind of information ... that forced us to intervene on the Balkans, contrary to all of our plans, which again resulted in the disastrous delay in the war with Russia...

We should have attacked Russia as from May 15th of 1941 and ... could have closed the campaign before the start of winter. Everything would have come out differently!

[...] I regret not having followed the sensibility which the brutal friendship with Italy prescribed[26]. The laws of life regrettably show that it is a mistake to accept anyone as equal in rank and quality if he really is not![27]

The uprising of the Colonial Peoples everywhere would have proclaimed that the awakening of the oppressed and exploited nations, the Egyptians, the Iraqi, the entire Near East, which had acclaimed German victories, would have had to be incited to a revolution:

---

[26] *Joachim Fest, HITLER – Eine Biografie. Publishing house Ullstein Buchverlage GmbH, Berlin, 10th edition [2008], p. 1047*

[27] *ibidem, p. 1047*

Not because of its aggressiveness or its lack of restraint will the Reich now go to ruins, but because of its incapability to radicalism, and its moral inhibitions: »think of our possibilities!« [...] *Life doesn't forgive any weaknesses!‹*[28]

It is to note, my Son", Immo's father continues after a short break and explains,

"Hitler could have incited the Muslims counting billions of people, in Indonesia and Malaysia, too, and possibly in addition also the peoples on the Indian subcontinent, to a joint war. On the other side, America could have found allies in South America, Central America, Africa and China!

That Hitler aimed at a war beyond the Second World War, again Joachim Fest states quite clearly:

*›The third position aspired by Hitler[29] was to cover the entire continent, but still have its nucleus of energy in Germany: The present mission of the Reich was to newly stimulate the tiring Europe and to use it as a reservoir of power for the **German World Rulership.** Hitler wanted to make up for the missed imperialistic phase of development of Germany and as latecomer to History achieve the largest possible price:*

»the dominance in Europe secured by the huge expansion of power in the East, and by dominance in Europe to secure dominance in the world«.

*Not entirely wrongfully did he assume, that the already divided Earth would soon no longer offer an opportunity to conquer an empire, and because always thinking in curt alternatives, he saw Germany compelled to either **found a world empire**, or »end its being as a second Netherlands or second Switzerland«, if not to »perish on this Earth or having to serve, as an enslaved people, the needs of others.« ‹*[30]

Thus Hitler's »Propaganda Specialists« have always talked of

---

[28] *ibidem, pp. 1047-1048*

[29] *With this Expression Hitler positions his own »Expansion of Power« between the »Soulless« capitalism of the Americans on the one side and the »inhuman« Russian Bolshevism on the other.*

[30] *Joachim Fest, HITLER – eine Biografie. Publishing house Ullstein Buchverlage GmbH, Berlin, 10th edition [2008], p. 1065*

*›[...] growing Werewolf Units and predicted a **War surmounting War** [...]‹[31],*

Which actually, in my understanding as a four-star general on »Tora«, indicates rather clearly, that all those nations on the Earth of the Humans, that had so far stayed friendly until 1945, where from now on to be mercilessly infested with the virus of war!

It is, my Son, not necessary to proceed hypothetically, because in 1944/45 mankind actually stood at the absolute abyss, immediately on the verge of their own destruction − and that after merely 200,000 years and not, as we »Toranians« did, only after several millions of years.

That exceedingly terrible 2nd World War, as is well known with its about 65,000,000 dead to be mourned, would have to be classified as a local confrontation of war, if Hitler had managed, with the help of Muslims, to instigate without transition a **3rd World War, meaning to cover the entire globe with the »fire of war«.**

The other side, the Americans, has shown toward the end of the war in 1945 that they were obviously not afraid of the destructive atomic power, having thoughtlessly thrown atom bombs on people in Hiroshima and Nagasaki, even though the Japanese were already practically defeated.

And consider, my Son, the Americans were the »good ones«! What could have happened if the »bad ones« with their »Fuehrer« Adolf Hitler would have come on the scene earlier? And no one will in the least doubt that Hitler Germany stood immediately before the completion of necessary missiles and the terrible »Bomb«!

Has Mussolini, the Italian prime minister and dictator, prevented Hitler from spreading a »**real World War**« across the entire globe?

Is Italy's »Duce«, the »Fuehrer« Mussolini, possibly the savior of mankind?

Must everyone today be thankful to the Italian Dictator that he, through his incompetence to wage wars, got Hitler not to incite the all-embracing wildfire with the help of the Muslim peoples?

---

[31] *ibidem, p. 1061*

The destruction of the majority of the population of the Earth after a development period of only 200,000 years would, of course, mean that the remaining inhabitants of Earth I would, in the case of further large disasters occurring, be **doomed**!

A fall-back on other celestial bodies would not have been possible for the remaining inhabitants of Earth, because necessary technical means were not yet available.

Because of our much further developed space technology, we »Toranians« could retreat to the Andromeda Galaxy and thus save the sparse remains of our people.

Thus we have come full circle:

The »Toranians« were, because of their overwhelming technology, many millions of years ago, in the position to take themselves to safety on a far distant planet and so to keep their species alive.

In 1945 though, by hairs' breadth mankind had destroyed itself, and that after only 200,000 years of existence:

Obviously the incompetence of an actually weak and insignificant minor Italian dictator and the loyalty to him of the far off »friend« in Berlin caused that the great and mighty, but megalomaniac German dictator did not eradicate the population of the Earth!

Now, my Son, towards the end of the phase of your studies, for which you had chosen the dictator Adolf Hitler, you could leisurely summarize everything in »two sentences«.

Thus ends the story of a young man they once called »Adi«:

A story, which »by the mark of evil« kept mounting from the child Adolf Hitler from Leonding (1898) to the adult Adolf Hitler in Berlin (1945) – to the absolute escalation with the complete doom of the German people.

A story in which the »spitefulness« of the German »Fuehrer« through murder of friends, murder of comrades, murder of his cousin, murder of priests, murder of Jews on to genocide, one day caught up with itself, because there was no more exacerbation of the term »evil«.

Do not forget the following events either, my Son, underlining very impressively the »mounting of evil«:

- The murder conspiracy around the »vassals« Goebbels, Himmler, Bormann and the execution of a murder by former SS member against the defenseless Hitler niece »Geli« Raubal , including knowledge by the own mother of the victim.

- The dastardly killing of the insignificant Lance Corporal Eugen Wasner with the help of the German »Wehrmacht«, led by Field Marshal Keitel.

- The order of the warlord Hitler, defeated on all fronts, to Albert Speer, his armament minister, in April **1945**, to punish his own people because it hadn't been capable of achieving the final victory over its overpowering opponents.

And a story around and about the »wise billy goat of Leonding« who surpassed himself on his »campaign of revenge« for the German dictator in the same period of time!

- Beginning with the bite of a domesticated animal, tortured and plagued with pain, into the penis of the nine-year old »Adi« on the meadow of rural Leonding in the year of **1898**, where »Adi« incited his playmates to the foul deed of piddling into the mouth of the animal.

- The devastating, to the deepest shameful »defeat« at the visit of the Jewish whore Rebecca in Vienna of the year **1908** – the first love adventure of the 19-year old Adolf Hitler.

- The rejection and escalating of contempt into unlimited hatred of his dearly loved niece »Geli« in **1931**.

- Two attempts of suicide of Eva Braun, Hitler's young companion, already as a young woman in **1932**, shortly after the death of »Geli« Raubal, and again in **1935**.

- Hitler's undignified death at the age of 56 in **1945** in the hard fought-over Berlin and consequently the doomed to failure plans of conquest and domination of the »world«!"

"I do thank you, Father, for this explicitly educational lecture with all its many interesting and for me as a student completely new pieces of information.

Even though you yourself practice the vocation as soldier, and haven't actually completed a university course of history, your way of describing historical events of overriding importance is so convincing that I am rather surprised. At university they cannot manage anything like that!

I am always astonished how you, Father, are capable of combining such complex contexts so that they become visible and understandable for everyone.

Thank you so much for everything, I will continue on it in my thoughts. The whole thing connects to our field tests, which now, after the »Episode Hitler« may put one in a pessimistic mood, wondering if mankind can really withstand such »pied pipers« in the future.

Still despite of all what I have learnt, a bit of melancholy creeps over me, thinking of the close connection between us »Toranians« and humans, which my studies have undoubtedly brought into daylight.

Because: It is all in all a pity, Father, that because of the validity of our large field tests, we are not permitted to talk about overall »world-wide« fears, nor about new and hopeful findings as well.

On the other hand, it is, considering the future, again consoling, because the day will surely come when we »Toranians« with all our knowledge and abilities may disclose our identity to the humans. I am really looking forward to that day, but – admittedly – I am slightly afraid of it, too, despite all of our superiority.".....

Loss of Homeland –
The scourge of war drives a completely innocent child of 4 years of age from the German Memel Territory in 1944/45

Adolf Hitler, you vile product of hell, who was it that authorized you to attack the Polish people, and thus provoke a World War?

Who authorized you to ambush the neighbouring countries of France, Netherlands, Belgium and Denmark and to carry the war far into the North to Norway, into the East to the Balkans and to the south into Africa?

The German People did not authorize you to those attacks on autonomous countries – The German People had merely with the help of President Hindenburg transferred to you the power of government – and that only within the limits of the then constitution!

But who authorized you, Adolf Hitler, to immediately after the transfer of power, to prohibit – everything that didn't suit you – parties, organizations, news papers, and to then perform terror and violence against your own people and all dissenters – especially against Jewish fellow citizens?

You, Adolf Hitler, wanted absolute power, focused on one person only – on yourself!

Soon you had that power at your disposal and used it to suppress whole peoples.

To this day, in the year 2012, it is not yet clear why the German people trusted you, a foreigner, and how you then were able to win from this people such a huge number of »Heil-Hitler-screamers« as tacit supporters.

Totally unsolved, too, is to this day, why especially »intelligent« people like academics, scholars, judges, doctors, teachers, priests, policemen, civil servants etc. supported you with all their might.

You, Adolf Hitler, rushed millions of young men and women no older than 19-, 20-, 21-years of age off to a murderous war, which they accepted willingly, yes, nearly enthusiastically taking part in the injustice of war.

Just to be mentioned in passing, it has not been clarified to this day, why the »intelligentsia«, which supported you nearly frenzied, didn't turn about when they realized, that they were serving murderous system of injustice.

Today we know, that you personally took ugly revenge on about 50,000 (in words: fifty thousand) dissenters with the help of show trials and obscene executions.[32]

You had von Stauffenberg, von Witzleben, and many others killed and frequently hung up on a meat hook like animals for slaughter, to rob them of even the last bit of human dignity.

The Lance Corporal Eugen Wasner, you dragged, you being the supreme warlord, before the army military court in Berlin, because he, the insignificant lance corporal had told is comrades on the east front a childhood story, a story in which the nine-year old

---

[32] *Der Spiegel, Ein Menschenleben gilt für nix, (A human life counts as nothing), Issue 43/1987*
and under www.spiegel.de/spiegel/print/d-13525519.html

Adolf Hitler, called »Adi« was bitten in the penis by a billy goat while urinating into the animal's mouth.

Eugen Wasner had to die under the guillotine towards the end of 1943, because he didn't move one inch from the truthfulness of this story!

Who has authorized you, Adolf Hitler, to deprive me, the four-year old Helmar Neubacher, of his home country?

I didn't vote for you in 1933, but still I was forced, under the protection of my mother in 1945 together with my two brothers, to leave my beloved Memelland in the outer eastern tip of the then German Reich, and flee in the ice-cold winter of 1945 from the charging Russian armies.

Three years ago, at the age of 68, I was allowed to once again see my former homeland Sakuten/ Easter Prussia/ District of Memel, today Lithuania.

On my parent's native soil two Lithuanian children were playing, a boy and a little girl, about three and a half to four and a half years old. The young, blonde mother told us, that they intended to build a little house on the land of my »Fathers«.

"Very good", I encouraged the mother in her idea,

"then »our farm« will again be filled with life."

All that was left to me were a few pieces of brick of my birthplace, a bit of »native soil« and the leaves of a chestnut tree which would have been planted by my parents – as a »last farewell«!

The old farm has become home to two little Lithuanian children, whereas this piece of luck for me, the »exiled«, has not been fulfilled for me in all those decades of my long life!

For myself personally, I have now come to the conclusion that in the last third of my life I am homeless!

The thought of homeland never occurred to me in that strange country Lithuania. Even with my parent's homestead in front of my eyes, of which nothing is left but an old barn, no mood of homeland arose in me. I felt very clearly that I had not arrived at »home«:

-   The land didn't belong to me.
-   I didn't have a Lithuanian passport.

- None of the water of that sea on that beautiful beach of Memel belonged to me.
- I supposedly didn't even have the right to breathe the clear air – everything was Lithuanian!

In all the many places where I had been on this beautiful Earth – everywhere I could have built myself a home:

- But home is not there where one coincidentally lives.
- No, home is on that piece of land which your heart has decided on!
- But the piece of land, to which my heart feels attached, is the little piece of land of my parents in the little village »Sakuten« in the District of Memel (in today's District of Klaipeda), if it became German once again.
- Thus is what could be »home« merely a fading memory.

I don't »owe« the loss of my homeland to the »bad« Russians, as I was intensely told for decades – no, the loss of my homeland I owe to you, Adolf Hitler.

You stretched your hand out for the oil fields in the far distant Caucasus and unlimited space for life in the East. In 1941 you ambushed the Russian people and carried an extremely bloody war into their country.

But you, insatiable tyrant, mad one decisive mistake which finally – thank God – led to your failure and downfall.

And when you, the former Austrian citizen who became German citizen only via the authorities in Braunschweig in 1933, managed to take prisoner several millions of Red Army soldiers, there was one thing that, in your presumptuousness, you hadn't considered: after your soldiers and the following Murder-SS had tormented the people and had unjustly taken possession of the vast land up to the River Volga, the totally unexpected happened:

- The oppressed Russian people were obviously already at the end of their strength in 1941/42, but then, like a miracle, the »Russian Bear« woke up – a true giant with huge strength was raised.
- And this giant, supported by the Russian winter, gave courage to the weak and exhausted people once more and bestowed it with new power.
- This actually already defeated people put you, Adolf Hitler, to flight, with their soldier in Stalingrad in January of 1943.

Unfortunately I too, as the four-year old Helmar, got to feel the terrible claws of the »Russian Bear« in 1944/45, when in the ice-cold winter of 1944/45 on covered wagons drawn by horses of Trakehnen breed, we had to leave our beloved homeland headlong in a miserable column of refugees. Because the »Russian Bear« was so furious and had suffered so many wounds by you, Hitler the aggressor, that he couldn't discern between guilty adult Germans and completely innocent children.

The blindly storming bear had one goal only: To catch the originator of all evil, Adolf Hitler, dug in and entrenched underground in his bunker in Berlin.

Who were you, Adolf Hitler? What were you? Were you a human being, were you a monster or still only a human monster?

Why were you, Adolf Hitler, so »evil«, that there couldn't be an exacerbation of the term »evil«?

Many authors and film makers in the past have tried to follow this question! But unfortunately until now, no one had been able to come anywhere near the answer to this question, let alone to answer it comprehensively.

Is there possibly the need of entirely new approaches, to tear the mask of the »mysterious« from your face, Adolf Hitler, behind which you had been hiding all your life?

Do authors have to tread entirely new paths in the future?

Can possibly book forms help which scientifically give reference for every quotation, and at the same time allow the author to implement a fictitious course of events which thus enable the authors, from the »birth« of the complete story, to employ his own imagination and evaluation in an unrestricted way?

As essence, the mythical »grimace« of the former »Fuehrer« of the Germans will, step by step, become more and more visible for everyone until perhaps in the end the secret around his »personality« is solved!

Especially well known authors like Joachim Fest, Jan Kershaw, Allan Bullock, and John Tolland have written biographies on you, Adolf Hitler, with the result: The thicker the books became the vaguer the face of the »demon« becomes.

One gets the idea, that J. Fest and his author colleagues have more in mind to write books which are comprehensive and complete using selected sources. Obviously in constant fear of their own critic colleagues telling them that something had been forgotten, everything, simply everything, in the way of information available is used.

The result: The »face« of Adolf Hitler becomes more and more blurred, more and more difficult to make out the thicker the book becomes. The face is distorted to a grimace and after 1000 pages it disappears entirely!

Still the Hitler biography by Joachim Fest is considered the standard work. And yet it must be criticized, that the famous author has neglected to sufficiently include the witnesses from the »Fuehrer's« shelter as sources for the downfall in 1945. Linge the servant, Traudl Junge the secretary, Misch the telephone operator and body guard had been in the vicinity of Hitler for years and that on a daily basis! They like no others could have been taken into consideration more strongly as witnesses of the times in J. Fest's biography, but one must consider this:

Even though all three of them had been thoroughly interrogated by Russians and Americans, they hadn't actually disclosed any »secrets«.

Even their books, which unfortunately appeared later than Fest's first edition, were written so much in general that I can't but suspect them to have kept secret the essentials from their superior's life. The »face« and especially all private life are kept in absolute darkness.

They, who experienced every fit of ecstasy and every outburst of rage quite perceptible from very close up, actually do not say anything – let alone anything negative about their employer. Obviously all three of them formed a close community beyond death with their »Fuehrer«!

Even if Traudl Junge at the end of her life states that she really couldn't understand how she could have become so »Hitler dependent«, it sounds to me to the highest extent dishonest.

Not even to the love life of their »icon« with Eva Braun do the »witnesses« say a clarifying or, moreover, a convincing word, even though not the least shade of that strange togetherness, due to the »physical nearness« to them, could have been kept hidden from them.

- Did Hitler have sex with Eva Braun?
- Was Hitler a homosexual, as has often been said?

- To which other women did he have sexual relationships?
- Was Hitler at all capable of performing the sexual act?
- Were his penis and /or testicles crippled or by the bite of the »billy goat of Leonding« in the year 1898 brutally altered?

Those people who should know best do not say anything – loyalty towards their »icon«, the »Fuehrer« is valued more than anything else.

Their loyalty beyond death is decisively responsible that the »Fuehrer« of the Germans face is to this day left in the dark – mysteriously transfigured.

In the case of a normal man, who is damaged for life, because his penis is disfigured and he thus is not capable to perform the best thing God has given a man – physical love and reproduction together with a woman – one could have pity.

But in the case of Hitler it is entirely different:
- Unnaturally deformed genitals can by all means be an explanation, because part of the reason, why Hitler presents himself to the world in such an evil way, that there can be no exacerbation for the term »evil«. In the case of the »human being« Hitler one can well talk about the reincarnation of evil, to be compared with the maliciousness of the devil!
- Hitler was a fanatic, brutal and unscrupulous – with these characteristics he brought us the 2nd World War, the biggest disaster of mankind with a number of about 65,000,000 dead!

It thus seems that especially the story of the billy goat of the nine-year old »Adi« from Leonding in the year of 1898, supplies a sure hint that there was something wrong with the sexual organs of the later adult Hitler!

- The »billy goat story« of which the insignificant lance corporal Eugen Wasner talked of, is comprehensively described in the book by his lawyer Güstrow »Tödlicher Alltag. Srafverteidiger im Dritten Reich« (Deadly Everyday Life. Counsel for the Defence in the Third Reich) … and Güstrow can most certainly, other than Linge, Junge and Mischke, be drawn up as an authentic source, because he was no vassal of the »Fuehrer«!

- He, Güstrow, defended Eugen Wasner before the Army Military Court in Berlin and accompanied his client on his last journey to the guillotine up to the door of the inner yard of Prison Ploetzensee.

It may be assumed, that fanaticism, brutality, and unscrupulousness must have already been present from birth in the genes of Adolf Hitler.

- Thus one cannot really hold the bite of the billy goat of Leonding to be the »root of all evil«.

- The bite of the billy goat may decisively have contributed to enhance the maliciousness of this person, because a mutilation of the penis would inevitably have led to the »long term winner« also becoming a »long term looser« – especially pertaining to the world of ladies and his own self-esteem.

That was shown by a special peculiarity, in those days visible to everyone:

- It was always noticeable that the »Fuehrer« of the Germans had a somewhat awkward appearance which strongly contradicted his demand for a staunch soldierly world view. It was clearly obvious that here was a case of a severe inferiority complex which then had to be compensated by malicious acts.

- This impression was also confirmed by the fact that Hitler used to stand around »awkwardly« in all kinds of situations. His hands then hung down thus, that one had to get the impression that with the palms of his hands one on top of the other, he wanted to protect his genitals.

It is high time that new authors, old and young, deal with the **Phenomenon »Adolf Hitler«** and his **»loyal surroundings«**. It must be today, it must be now – not tomorrow! Because tomorrow it may be too late.

- Today there are only **few** who participated actively in the 2nd World War.

- **Many** who were the children born in the times of war and

- **very many** »sincere« citizens who show interest in those times gone by!

»Brown mentality«, even today, 2012, again being perceived increasingly, one cannot forbid, and by no means by employing surveillance by secret services. Rightist mentality must be overpowered by argumentation of those true to the state, which fortunately do exist in numbers of millions to this day.

But tomorrow, it may be too late, because the face of Hitler doesn't only become blurred in biographies of historians, but increasingly in the minds of our youths who, in the meantime, follow entirely different interests.

Recently I saw on television how a Jewish lady, who in 1945 had survived the Concentration Camp of Auschwitz, thinks about it today:

Although she and her twin sister having been brutally tormented by the SS-doctor Mengele, the »Angel of Auschwitz«, and her father and mother murdered in the camp, she forgave the beast Mengele.

I, Helmar Neubacher, here beg of the Lord to deal with the matter in the ways of the Old Testament – an eye for an eye and a tooth for a tooth – and not like those fellow citizens of Semitic Faith in their magnanimity to forgive.

At least for that monster Hitler, may providence which he so often had implored, pay him back for simply everything to the last generation. The vision of the biblical hell may be appropriate for this man, to obtain for his victims a small degree of satisfaction. His lack of understanding, his abuse hurled at his already severely by war injured people, shall be reason enough to only forgive him, after he has though purification by infernal punishment, come to his senses and attained honest remorse. The same goes for his innumerable accomplices.

The Author

Nazi Rule –
A Regime of Terror

All in all, in the twelve years, three months and nine days in which the »1000-year Reich« existed, the self appointed »Fuehrer« of the Germans had about 50,000 (in words: fifty thousand) men and women murdered, who did not follow his opinion – resistance fighters, oppositionals, and whoever doubted the »Final Victory«.

At this point, well known, brave soldiers are listed who were participants to the attempt on Hitler's life on July the 20th, 1944.

They lost their lives through sentencing to death and subsequent execution, execution by firing squad under martial law or suicide.

They are listed standing in for the ranks of murdered opponents to the Nazis – may their names help to keep the memory of those 50,000 awake who gave their lives for others.

- Colonel General ret. Ludwig Beck, executed by firing squad

- Lieutenant Colonel Robert Bernardis, executed

- Major Hans-Jürgen Graf von Blumenthal, executed

- Lieutenant Colonel Hasso von Boehmer, executed

- Admiral Wilhelm Kanaris, executed

- Captain Max-Ulrich Graf von Drechsel, executed

- Lieutenant Colonel Karl-Heinz Engelhorn, executed

- Lieutenant Colonel Otto Erdmann, executed

- General Erich Fellgiebel, executed

- Colonel Eberhard Finckh, executed

- Colonel General Friedrich Fromm, executed by firing squad

- Captain Ludwig Gehre, executed

- Lieutenant Werner von Haeften, executed by firing squad

- Reserve Lieutenant Albrecht von Hagen, executed

- Colonel Kurt Hahn, executed

- Colonel Georg Hansen, executed

- Lieutenant General Paul von Hase, executed

- Major Egbert Hayessen, executed

- Major General Otto Herfurth, executed

- Colonel General Erich Hoepner, executed

- Major Roland von Hößlin, executed

- Lieutenant Colonel Caesar von Hofacker, executed

- Colonel Friedrich Gustav Jäger, executed

- Reserve Captain Jens Jessen, executed

- Lieutenant Colonel Bernhard Klamroth, executed
- Reserve Major Hans Georg Klamroth, executed
- Captain Friedrich Karl Klausing, executed
- Major Gerhard Knaak, executed
- Lieutenant Colonel Fritz von Lancken, executed
- Major Ludwig Freiherr von Leonrod, executed
- General Fritz Lindemann, executed by firing squad
- Colonel Hans-Ottfried von Linstow, executed
- Colonel Rudolf Graf von Marogna-Redwitz, executed
- Colonel Joachim Meichßner, executed
- Lieutenant Colonel Ernst Munzinger, executed by firing squad
- Major Hans-Ulrich von Oertzen, suicide
- General Friedrich Olbricht, executed by firing squad
- Major General Hans Oster, executed
- Colonel Albrecht Ritter Mertz von Quirnheim, executed by firing squad
- General Dr. Friedrich von Rabenau, executed by firing squad
- Lieutenant Colonel Karl Ernst Rathgens, executed
- Colonel Alexis Freiherr von Roenne, executed
- Fieldmarshal General Erwin Rommel, suicide
- Judge General Karl Sack, executed
- Lieutenant Colonel Joachim Sadrozinski, executed
- Major Hans-Viktor von Salviati, executed
- Major Adolf Friedrich von Schack, executed
- Colonel Hermann Schöne, executed
- Reserve Cavalry Captain Friedrich Scholz-Babisch, executed
- Reserve Lieutenant Colonel Fritz-Detlof Graf von der Schulenberg, executed
- Colonel Georg Schulze-Büttger, executed

- Captain Ulrich-Wilhelm Graf Schwerin von Schwanefeld, executed

- Lieutenant Colonel Günther Smend, executed

- Major General Hans Emil Otto von Sponeck, executed by firing squad

- Colonel Claus Graf Schenk von Stauffenberg, executed by firing squad

- Major General Helmuth Stieff, executed

- General Karl-Heinrich von Stülpnagel, executed

- Lieutenant General Fritz Thiele, executed

- Major Busso Thoma, executed

- Lieutenant General Karl Freiherr von Thüngen, executed

- Lieutenant Colonel Gerd von Tresckow, suicide

- Lieutenant Colonel Hans-Alexander von Voss, suicide

- Reserve Lieutenant Peter York von Wartenburg, executed

- Fieldmarshal Genral Erwin von Witzleben, executed

- Lieutenant General Gustav von Zielberg, executed by firing squad.

This list is not complete. Further names of victims of revenge of the attempted assassination of the 20th of July, 1944, you will e.g. find under

- Hans-Albert Hoffmann, Die Deutsche Heeresführung im 2.Weltkrieg, Steffen Verlag (2011), Pp.152/153
  (The German Supreme Command oft the Army during World War II)

- www.denkmalprojekt.org/Gedenkbuecher/gb_20_Juli_44.htm
  (Memorial project/memorial books)

- http://www.gedenkstaette-ploetzensee.de/02_dt.html
  (Memorial site Ploetzensee)

When in Berlin, please do visit the Memorial Site Plötzensee. Here Hitler had 2891 opponents and critics of the regime executed from 1933 to 1945.

This book was written in honour of Lance Corporal Eugen Wasner, born in Leonding, Austria.

Eugen Wasner didn't move the slightest bit from the truthfulness of a story he told his comrades in arms on the Eastern Front in 1943.

According to this, the nine-year old »Adi« was bitten in the penis by a billy goat while urinating into its mouth.

Eugen Wasner was the one to know – he and his school friend Bruno Kneisel assisted in this foul deed in 1898.

Eugen Wasner was condemned to death through the guillotine by the Army Military Court in Berlin via his former school friend, Adolf Hitler, for demoralization of armed forces and insult to the »Fuehrer«.

The »Fuehrer« and Chancellor of the Reich thus took terrible revenge on his »most insignificant soldier« – an unreasonably high price for a childhood story!

»I have never for a moment doubted the content of truth of Wasner's report who was a naïve though deeply pious person"[33], writes Dietrich Güstrow (real name Dietrich Wilde), who defended Eugen Wasner before the Army Military Court in Berlin as his lawyer and who accompanied the condemned man on his last journey to the guillotine up to the door of the execution yard of Berlin-Plötzensee.

A personal request of the author:

For a possible new edition of this book I would very much like to publish a picture of Eugen Wasner in his honour.

I thus ask relatives and acquaintances of Eugen Wasner from Leonding to make a picture from those times available to me.

---

[33] *Dietrich Güstrow, Tödlicher Alltag. Strafverteidiger im Dritten Reich, publishing house Severin und Siedler [1981], p. 144*

(Deadly Everyday Life: Counsel to the Defence during the Third Reich)

CHILDREN in FAMINE
To HELP also brings satisfaction to those who Help!

Please do read the next page, too.

On expensive bikes made of carbon fibre we race along the countryside,

- enjoying our lovely nature on chromium blinking choppers
- go on holidays in big flashy cars bragging with excessive horse power
- cruise on the seas with sailing- and motor yachts
- fly in God's own sky in sports aircraft

… and all of that just for the fun of it!

On the other hand, every three seconds a human child dies because it hasn't got anything to drink or to eat.

Tsunamis, earthquakes and other disasters caused by us ourselves enhance this unspeakable suffering – and just about bring this »ball« which we boastfully call »World«, but because of its tininess and susceptibility also give the name »Earth«, to its breaking point!

Let's carry on enjoying our well earned prosperity, but at the same time let us open our hearts for the enormous suffering and great injustice right here in front of our own doorstep!

Let us change from TALKING to DOING!!!

For this purpose I have asked myself two questions:

1. How do I position my present life situation on a scale of state of mind?

   - excellent
   - satisfactory
   - reasonably well
   - bad/poor.

2. Can I spare anything for those who do not even have enough food or drink?

The evaluation for my own position on the scale results in:
excellent.

That is why I am going to donate 25% of my author's royalties from every book sold, to children caught in famine.

I ask of all people to also pose the Questions 1 and 2 to themselves, and, after an honest answer, to find a path to a donation account.

With heartfelt thanks, Yours H. Neubacher, Author.

Acknowledgements

Illustration on front cover:
- Photo of a prepared billy goat skull
- Domestic goat: capra aegagrus hircus
- The skull is in the possession of the author

Illus. 4:
- Altered scetch from:

    Gudrun Pausewang, Adi – Jugend eines Diktators,
    (Adi – Youth of a Dictator)
    Ravensburger Buchverlag, [1997], S. 6

    and

    August Kubizek, Adolf Hitler – Mein Jugendfreund,
    (Adolf Hitler – A Friend from my Youth)
    Leopold Stocker Verlag, Graz [1953], S. 112/113

Foto on Page 142:
- With friendly permission of N. Khoyun, Island of Sylt, Germany

All other illustrations by the author.

Website: www.pyramidenbau-aegypten.de
Email: info@pyramidenbau-aegypten.de
Website: www.schaduf-book.de
Email: info@schaduf-book.de